RIOT

*To Gail,
who also loves words!
May you be blessed with
writing your own books
someday soon.*

MARY CASANOVA

*So glad to meet you!
Peace to you in all
you pursue*

*Mary Casanova
1996*

HYPERION BOOKS FOR CHILDREN

D1410001

For my parents, who demonstrate love through
their words and deeds . . .
and for Bill Elliot and the law-enforcement
officers who braved the storm

Text © 1996 by Mary Casanova.

All rights reserved. No part of this book may be reproduced or transmitted in any form
or by any means, electronic or mechanical, including photocopying, recording, or by
any information storage and retrieval system, without written permission from the pub-
lisher. For information address Hyperion Books for Children, 114 Fifth Avenue,
New York, New York 10011-5690.

Printed in the United States of America.

First Edition

1 3 5 7 9 10 8 6 4 2

This book is set in 12-point Times Roman.

Designed by Joann Hill-Lovinski.

Library of Congress Cataloging-in-Publication Data
Casanova, Mary.
Riot / Mary Casanova—1st ed.
p.   cm.
Summary: When his father engages in vandalism against nonunion employees,
Bryan, a sixth grader, must decide whether to accept his father's actions
or do what he believes is right.
ISBN 0-7868-0215-4 (trade)—ISBN 0-7868-2204-X (lib. bdg.)
[1. Fathers and sons—Fiction. 2. Labor disputes—Fiction.]
I. Title.
PZ7.C266Ri 1996
[Fic]—dc20   96-6890

MARY CASANOVA is a fiscal-year-1995 recipient of a fellowship in literature from the Arrowhead Regional Arts Council, through funds provided by the McKnight Foundation.

CHAPTER ONE

Weeds poke up through the gravel-covered field, and the rows of yellow mobile homes are gone. It's been a year since everything broke loose, since black clouds of putrid smoke chugged into the sky, defying the efforts of fire-fighters. I bike here often, turning it all over in my mind, replaying the events like a videotape, forcing myself to remember. Remembering helps me to understand—not only what happened to our town, but to me.

After Communion, Bryan Grant folded his hands casually—a sixth grader couldn't look too serious—and walked back to the third pew, where his family sat every Sunday.

Nearing the scrolled edge of the wooden pew, Bryan felt a warm hand on his shoulder. He looked behind. It was Dad, biceps outlined beneath his denim shirt, sleeves rolled up, jaw clenched. With a slight sideways nod, Dad signaled toward the back of the church.

Bryan glanced at the empty foyer. Why would Dad want him to leave early?

Mom sat in the pew, her blue dress skimming her knees, with the seven-year-old twins, Josh and Elissa. She tapped the space beside her, signaling Bryan to sit.

He hated when his parents did this, pulling him in two directions. All summer long, it seemed he couldn't please one without upsetting the other.

The sound of shuffling feet blended with the choir's music, "Those who trust in the Lord will gain new strength, they will rise on the wind like the eagle. . . ."

Bryan hesitated a moment. Then deliberately avoiding his mother's eyes, he followed Dad down the side aisle toward the red exit sign. The church was packed with locals, tourists, and nonunion workers. With each step, heads turned.

Bryan's face grew hot. Why should he feel embarrassed? After all, he was just doing what his dad wanted.

At the back of the church, kneeling at the end of the last pew, one girl caught his attention. He'd never seen *her* before. She glanced up at him—long chestnut hair, peach-colored skin, and hazel eyes flecked gold—and smiled.

A smile like a whisper only he could hear.

Then, quickly, she looked away.

Bryan stopped breathing. A rush of tingling warmth climbed to his neck and face, and then he passed by. He'd probably stared a second too long and made a fool of himself. Girls didn't do much for him, not the way they did to Kyle. But this girl . . . she was . . . well, perfect. And she'd smiled right at him. And he hadn't even tried to smile back. What an idiot! Slowing his step, he glanced up at the vaulted ceiling. Who was she? Please God, let her be in my class Wednesday.

Dad nudged Bryan's shoulder from behind, passed ahead of him through the double wooden doors, and stormed down the stone slab steps.

Sliding his hands deep in his pockets, Bryan followed his father toward the parking lot. It was September 3, and the sun shone high in the sky, summertime hot. Under Bryan's white T-shirt, a bead of sweat stole down his back and stopped at his Levi's.

He trailed Dad through the parking lot to Mom's red minivan, which she had insisted they take to church. She'd bought it for her long drives to Bemidji to complete her teaching degree—although now she taught in town. The pickup suited Dad better.

"Hop in," Dad said, his voice strained.

Bryan jumped in on the passenger side and closed the door. Had he done something wrong? What was going on, anyway? The warm air hung between them. Bryan cranked down the window.

He glanced at the passenger mirror, at his slate-green eyes and the few light freckles across his nose. His auburn hair was darker than the girl's, more like the crayon color "burnt sienna." If he had to name her hair, he'd call it apricot. He ran his forefinger back and forth above his upper lip. Before long, he'd probably feel stubble growing, but not yet.

"We have a few minutes before church lets out," Dad said, stroking his short, dark mustache.

"Yeah?" Bryan waited for an explanation.

"I just couldn't sit there," Dad said, shoving the key into the ignition, "and watch those rats file up for Communion in my church. Isn't it enough that they take away our jobs?"

"Rat" was the name for anyone who worked for Badgett Construction, the nonunion contractor chosen by Gold Paper Portage to build the new paper-machine project.

Mom hated the word "rat," but then as a teacher, she was ultrasensitive to any name-calling. She shook her head at lots of Great-grandpa Howie's words, too. Grandpa talked about how he used to have nightmares of getting wrapped up in the old plant's paper rollers. Now the new machine, costing some $535 million, would stretch more than a couple of city blocks. Incredible.

"Where are we going?" Bryan asked.

"You'll see."

Was the girl a rat? Were her parents "scabs," here to build the new paper machine and then move on to another town? Maybe. Maybe not. Probably just tourists from Chicago or Iowa, coming north for a week of fishing on Rainy Lake.

As Dad gunned the engine, the van spewed gravel and Bryan jolted back in his seat.

"Things are going to start changin', Bry." Dad gripped the wheel with both hands and zipped past the library and the courthouse. "When school starts, you stay away from those rats, okay?" There was an edge to his voice.

"Why?" Bryan asked.

"They're dangerous, that's why. Most of them carry knives in their boots—and they'll use them, too." He glanced at Bryan. "Comes from living on the road so much, going from job to job like nomads."

Bryan tried to picture knife fights breaking out at his elementary school. Maybe that could happen in New York, but not in northern Minnesota, not in Blue Ash.

They turned the corner, past the enormous statue of Smokey Bear, and headed toward the paper mill. Dwarfing the downtown, the mill sat on the edge of Rainy River next to the dam where, a hundred years earlier, a waterfall had flowed. The paper mill spouted steam and smoke into the blue cloudless sky. Though the air in town didn't always smell bad, today it stunk.

"Smells like a ripe outhouse," Bryan said.

"That's what money smells like," Dad answered, repeating the common refrain.

One block north of Main Street, against the towering blue backdrop of the mill, a few dozen men carried white picket signs. One sign showed a black rat in the center of a circle with a diagonal line slashed across it. Others read: BADGETT—NO WAY! SCABS ARE A DISEASE, and RATS GO HOME!

Dad leaned out the window. "Hey!"

"Coming to join us, Stan?" one guy yelled.

"Bring some coffee?" said another.

"Coffee?" someone shouted. "How about beer?" Laughter followed.

Clustered together, the men wore caps, T-shirts, and jeans. Some were white-haired; others were younger than Bryan's dad.

"Just stopping for a minute," Dad said. "Well? What have you heard?"

The men looked at one another. A short, pudgy man with a Twins T-shirt shrugged. He stepped up to the van, put his speckled hand on Dad's arm, and, his eyebrows wiggling like black and white caterpillars over his nose, glanced over at Bryan. The man lowered his voice.

"It's going to happen, Stan," he said. "Are you with us?"

"You bet I am!" Dad said. He swore. "Think I'm going to let those rats take away our jobs without a fight?"

Bryan looked out his window toward the city tennis

5

courts. Dad didn't usually swear—only a few times, when he'd hit his thumb with a hammer. *What* was going to happen?

"Do you have a plan yet?" Dad asked.

Bryan glanced back.

The man raised his eyebrows. He forced a smile at Bryan, but his eyes were somber. "Later, Stan. We better talk later."

Dad threw open the car door, hopped out, and slapped the man on the back. "I think we better talk now."

The two men joined the picketers. Bryan watched Dad blend with the crowd. The morning sun fell on his shaggy dark hair; he'd been on the lines every day all summer and hadn't had time to trim it. Dad wasn't a quitter.

Bryan remembered Dad's words in the arena locker room, before he'd coached the Squirts to their hockey tournament win last season. "Don't hold back because you're afraid," Dad had said, "or you'll get hurt out there." He scanned the room and his thread-line scar, which ran from above his right eye to the top of his cheekbone, like a hero's medal, emphasized his point. Dad knew what it was to push hard. He had looked every boy in the eye, especially his top players, Bryan and Kyle. "Skate hard! Do your best! And save your fear for after the game."

Sitting up straighter, Bryan crossed his arms over his chest. This labor dispute was like a tournament game, only it wasn't over winning a shiny gold trophy, it was over jobs.

"Rats," Bryan said under his breath, "ruining our whole town!" It felt good to say it. It made him feel like he was standing right alongside Dad, fighting the fight with him, even if he didn't fully understand the battle.

6

By the time Dad climbed back in the van and they pulled up to the church, the parking lot was empty. Mom was sitting on the cement entry steps, waiting with the blond-haired twins.

She wasn't smiling.

CHAPTER TWO

The twins rode in the middle seat and Bryan sat in back, his arms stretched across the crimson seat. As they approached the driveway, Mom pushed the garage-door opener that was clipped to the visor. She shook her head. "Stan," she said, "I don't like what's going on."

In the visor mirror, her eyes caught Bryan's for an instant, holding him, as if she needed him for support. Bryan looked out his window and pretended to study the neighbor's lawn. The van pulled up the sloped driveway.

Inside the garage, Dad turned off the key. He sat there while the twins unbuckled. "Nobody likes what's going on, Meg," he said. "Nobody."

"Let's keep our family out of it," Mom whispered. "Please."

Bryan, glad to escape, hopped out of the minivan. He stepped out of the garage to the backyard and climbed into the woven hammock under the willow tree, its long, slender leaves a canopy of flickering green. The minute he closed his eyes, Gretsky, his gray miniature schnauzer, pushed his black nose through the mesh hammock and licked Bryan's arm.

"C'mon up," Bryan said and hoisted Gretsky's sixteen pounds up beside him.

The garden hose swooshed as Dad pulled it across the grass toward the blue spruce saplings bordering the yard.

Bryan tried to relax, but he couldn't. Something beyond his understanding was brewing, both with the strikers and between his parents. It was as though he were watching storm clouds form on the edge of the horizon.

Squinting, he glanced up through the leaves. The sky was perfectly blue. Almost as perfect as that girl's smile.

"Bry," Dad called. "The hose is all tangled. Would you please give me a hand?"

"Sure." Bryan climbed out of the hammock, set Gretsky down, and straightened the twisted hose.

Then he crossed the lawn and deck to the sliding doors and stepped inside the house, his dog following. He sat down at the piano. The smell of lunch floated from the kitchen into the living room. Bryan could almost taste Mom's grilled ham and cheese sandwiches.

Striking only the white keys, he played a progression of slow chords—C, A, F, and G—with his left hand. Deep notes, almost like an electric bass guitar. He thought of going to the beach later with Kyle and of the girl's apricot hair, and his tempo quickened. He added a right-hand melody, making up a tune as he went.

The glass door from the deck slid open. "Am I the only one who works around here?" Dad's voice was stern.

Bryan stilled his hands on the keys. His stomach tightened. He hated the way he cowered at his dad's voice, almost like a puppy with its tail between its legs. Maybe with time, as he grew older, he'd be able to hold his own.

"Stan," Mom called from the kitchen. "It's Sunday.

There really isn't much to do right now. The table's already set, and I was enjoying Bryan's music."

From the corner of his eye, Bryan watched Dad walk around the cutting block in the center of the kitchen, pause, and slip his arm around Mom's waist, which was bare between her gray aerobics shorts and cropped top.

Bryan pretended to be invisible.

Dad kissed Mom on the cheek.

"Stan, maybe you should start exercising," she said. Since she'd started working out, she had made it her job to get everybody in shape. "It might help you feel better . . . get rid of some of that tension."

"No time," he said and headed back outside. "Besides," he added through the screen door, "I'm already a Greek god." He laughed and turned away.

Mom smiled. "You're impossible."

Bryan exhaled deeply, his shoulders relaxed. He looked at Gretsky, flopped lifeless on the green couch, paws toward the ceiling. *He* certainly didn't have to worry about labor disputes.

"Go ahead. Keep playing," Mom said to Bryan. She wiped her hands on a kitchen towel. "Don't worry about Dad. He's just tense right now."

"Nah," Bryan answered, standing up. "I don't feel like it anymore."

He kneeled next to the couch and stroked Gretsky's clipped coat and head, his soft, shaggy underbelly. The dog groaned contentedly and licked Bryan's hand with his pink tongue. Imitating his dad's voice, Bryan whispered in Gretsky's ear, "Don't you ever work around here?"

Then he rose and walked to the end of the hall where he shared a bedroom with Josh. He climbed the ladder to the top bunk, straightened the blue and green star quilt grandma Effie had made last Christmas, and climbed down. He tossed his basketball into the closet and picked up Josh's Lego blocks from the floor. At least Dad couldn't complain about his room.

Straddling the stool next to the long table at the window, he looked outside at the wooden playset that Dad had made. Josh swung slowly from rung to rung like a sloth. Elissa was on the ground, sticking leaves and twigs into the top of a sand mound.

Next to the cedar fence, where the marigolds were fiery gold, yellow, and orange, Dad was digging up weeds and tossing them over his shoulder into a withered heap on the lawn.

Bryan hooked his heels on the stool and watched his father. How could he, a twelve year old, help? Maybe there was a way. He reached for the blue and white ceramic jar he'd made a month ago at College for Kids, pulled out a pen, and rolled it between his fingers. He ripped out a sheet of notebook paper, then wrote:

Dear Editor,
My dad is an electrician and a very hard worker. He's a union worker and should get the work to build the new paper machine. My dad doesn't want to leave town to find work! I say, no way to Badgett Construction!
Sincerely,
Bryan Grant

He reread his letter, then added after his name, "Sixth Grader."

After lunch, with a towel draped around his neck, a

Hornets cap snugged backward over his hair, and a blue backpack over his shoulders, Bryan rolled down his driveway on his ten-speed and glided half a block to a small cedar-sided house.

Kyle Kalowski stepped out the front door and saluted. He was taller than Bryan by a couple of inches, with wider shoulders and blond tangled hair. "Hi, Bry! I'm coming."

Bryan waved back. He'd been friends with Kyle since before he could remember. Their mothers had met at the hospital the last week in September when both boys were born. Kyle and Bryan were always the oldest in their class, something that hadn't hurt them on the hockey team.

Kyle grabbed his green bike from the side of his garage with one hand, and with the other he pretended to throw a ball into the hoop over the garage door. "Thank you, thank you," he called. "Skip the applause!"

Bryan shouted, "You're such a screwball!" He pushed down his pedal and headed south.

Kyle followed. "Hey, the beach isn't this way!"

"I know. There's something I want to do first."

At the end of the block, Bryan stopped at the blue mailbox, pulled a white envelope from under his shirt, and opened the door with a squeak. The letter slipped down. It was on its way to the *Daily News*. If the paper printed it, Dad would be surprised when he read through the editorials. At least he'd know his son was on his side.

Bryan turned right, shifted gears, and rode side by side with Kyle. He felt strong inside, older somehow. A good feeling.

A white-throated sparrow sang its melancholy song. A grasshopper, clacking, flew across the road, just missing Bryan's front tire.

"So, what's up now?" Kyle asked.

"I'm thinking. . . ." said Bryan, the sun hot on his face. But he kept on pedaling, following the asphalt road, which wound between stands of aspen trees, leaves beginning to turn yellow, fluttering in the breeze. The field beyond the woods, where Bryan and Kyle used to catch bugs, was covered with acres of freshly laid gravel and enclosed by a ten-foot-high chain-link fence. Inside, row upon row of canary-yellow mobile homes housed hundreds of Badgett workers, who rode charter buses to work at the mill.

In a small metal building at the camp entrance, some-one moved. A guard. Dad had talked about how he couldn't stand the Badgett Construction guards. "Hired bulldogs," he'd called them. Bryan suddenly had an idea.

He slowed his bike to a stop on the far side of the street. "Grab a few rocks," he said.

"Why?" Kyle screwed up his face, not moving his hands off his handlebars.

"You'll see," Bryan said. He reached down, pretended to scratch his ankle, picked up five stones, and handed two to Kyle. "When I say 'now,' nail the guardhouse."

"Wait a second," Kyle said.

"Now!" Bryan let his stones fly, one at a time. His aim was good. Ting! Ting! Crack!

"Go!" he yelled, forcing his foot down on his right pedal. He glanced back. Red-faced, Kyle was pumping hard, hunched over his handlebars. In the distance, the guard flew out of the house holding a clear, four-foot riot shield in front of his wide shoulders and angry face. He ran after them, shouting.

CHAPTER THREE

"Hey, you punks!" the guard bellowed. "Get back here!"

Their bike tires whirred over pavement. Bryan raced past the stop sign, spun around the corner, and turned right onto Highway 11, heading toward the center of town. His lungs burned, but he gripped his handlebars tightly and pedaled faster. Kyle sped behind him.

When they were a half mile away, Bryan slowed down until he and Kyle rode side by side.

"We hit the guardhouse!" Bryan said, struggling to catch his breath. "I can't believe it. We actually hit it!"

Kyle lifted one hand from his handlebar and flung his stones into the ditch.

Bryan glanced at Kyle. "You mean . . . you didn't throw any?"

Kyle shook his head. "What if that guard caught us? He'd have pounded us! What's the point?"

"Why couldn't you just go along with it? No one got hurt or anything," Bryan said in annoyance. "And it was just for fun," he added, aware that it was somehow more than that.

Usually Bryan and Kyle thought the same way about everything: They both loved watermelon, tortilla chips and hot sauce, biking, and hockey. They even had the same favorite book—*Hatchet*.

They biked past the high-school track field.

"Hey," Bryan said, "maybe you don't get it because your parents didn't grow up here." Kyle's parents were from Grand Rapids, a few hours away, and they went back there lots of weekends to visit. "Look, my parents, grandparents, and great-grandparents are all from here."

"So?" Kyle screwed up his face, clearly not getting Bryan's point.

"Oh, forget it. Maybe you'll never get it."

Kyle looked straight ahead. "No," he said, his voice shaky. "I don't get it!"

Kyle was usually lots of fun, the class joker. Was he trying to make Bryan feel guilty? Actually Bryan felt good about what he'd done. Until now, the most daring thing he'd ever risked was toilet papering the Stassons' house on Halloween last year, but he and Kyle had gotten caught in the act. They'd spent the following Sunday on ladders removing every white speck from the limbs. Kyle hadn't minded. It was a chance to get close to Laura Stasson, whom Kyle had loved passionately back then. Now he'd forgotten she even existed.

Bryan adjusted his backpack strap, which was cutting into his shoulder. He didn't know why he had nailed the guard's building, not exactly, but it felt good—really good— like slamming a surprise shot into the opponent's net.

Besides, if the guard had caught him, Bryan knew Dad would have understood. Still, Bryan hated when he and Kyle disagreed. To shift the talk away from the guard at the housing camp, Bryan told Kyle about the girl at church and how she'd smiled at him.

The boys pedaled past stores and banks, the paper mill, and the American and Canadian flags flying at the end of Main Street. They rumbled over shipping-yard railway tracks and passed under a three-foot-round pipe that ran from enormous woodchip piles to the mill. The pipe wheezed, sucking in the chips like a giant vacuum cleaner. A loaded logging truck roared past them; from its longest log, a red ribbon whipped in the wind.

"This girl," Kyle said, "did she smile just a little, or was it a great big smile?"

"I said, 'She smiled.'" Bryan told him. "Just a smile. It's no big deal. Really."

"Right. Look straight at me and say that," said Kyle, his sun-bleached eyebrows arching.

On the bike trail, the boys passed the pulp-wood storage yard, where tree-length logs were stacked as far as Bryan could see, stockpiled to be made into paper. Beyond that, the shipping yard was filled with what resembled a giant's toys—pipes and bolts and boxes and cylinders of every color—building parts for the goliath paper machine.

"In Grand Rapids," Kyle commented, "the mill has gardens surrounding it. It's pretty."

"Oh," Bryan said. Well, this wasn't Grand Rapids.

Ten minutes later, they turned at the twenty-foot statue of a voyageur, an early fur trader who traveled the northern lakes and rivers by canoe. At the beach, they locked their ten-speeds in the metal rack.

Bryan breathed in the water-scented air. Three miles from the mill the air smelled fresher. All the tension in town seemed left behind them for a while.

"C'mon, let's go," Bryan said, walking toward the

lake. A dozen kids and parents were spread out on the stretch of sand, a haze hanging in the air over them. Under an arching pavilion, a family gathered. The sand beach radiated a wave of heat.

The lifeguard, short and muscular, climbed the steps of the purple and gold painted platform. "Last day," she called as the boys scattered seagulls on their way to the dock.

Bryan took off his backpack, set it on the weathered boards, and pulled out a small, black video camera. He was glad Mom had finally agreed to let him take it to the beach so he and Kyle could tape the dives they'd worked on all summer. Since she had gotten it last Christmas, she'd guarded it like a diamond. "It's for capturing moments with my most valuable jewels," she'd said, kissing him on the cheek. "Mom," he'd groaned. She was like that.

"Here's the plan," Bryan said. "You dive, I shoot. I dive, you shoot me."

"Really? Sounds dangerous." Kyle's face was unflinching.

Bryan tilted his head. "You know what I mean."

By late morning, Bryan had nearly perfected his back dive and his forward one-and-a-half. He stood on the edge of the diving platform, looking back at Kyle, who held the camera.

"This one," Kyle announced, "executed with tremendous skill, will undoubtedly qualify young Mr. Grant for the Olympics."

"Yeah, right," Bryan said. He bent his knees, swept his arms low, then brought them upward. As he did, he caught sight of the girl with apricot hair, wearing a turquoise swimsuit, stepping wide around a sunbather. She was walking down the dock, coming closer.

17

"Folks," Kyle announced, "he's losing his concentration."

"Kyle," Bryan whispered loudly, "that's her!"

"Her as in *her*?" Kyle said, turning his head slightly.

"She's coming down the dock!"

Bryan started teetering on the edge of the board. He dug his toes in, swung his arms in wide circles, but started falling, and with his arms and feet pointed skyward, torpedoed into a mighty back flop. Slaaap!!! He went under and contemplated swimming under the dock and hiding, but he didn't. In the brisk water, he surfaced, skin stinging, and wiped water from his eyes. He stretched out his arms and floated on his back. He didn't feel like getting out.

When he looked up, the girl was at the end of the diving platform. Bryan couldn't believe this. Could this be happening to him? "Could y'all move out of the way?"

Y'all? Bryan looked around. Nobody from Minnesota said y'all. With a sick feeling, he realized that she was probably here with Badgett Construction. His heart sank. He couldn't let himself like her. He couldn't. Dad would kill him.

Bryan breaststroked to the ladder, started climbing, and stopped halfway. He turned and watched.

The girl walked to the edge of the board. Looking down at her feet, she positioned her heels over the edge, her calves round and muscular. In one fluid motion, she pressed her arms down, reached up, and set them in a perfect T, then arched into a graceful back dive. Gliding through the air, she cut into the dark water, leaving a string of sparkling beads behind her.

Bryan could hardly breathe. Not only was she pretty, but she could really dive!

18

She surfaced, brushed water from her eyes, and swam toward him. "Hey, I saw you at church," she said, smiling. "You were leaving early."

Before he could say a word, Kyle stepped toward the ladder, focusing the video camera on the girl. "That was great," he said. "Nice dive."

Bryan climbed onto the gray, weathered dock. He'd already made a fool of himself by hanging back, staring again. She probably thought he was a brainless geek by now. He turned and watched her.

"Thanks," she said, wet bangs in her eyes. She dipped her head back in the water and lifted it out again. "This water's freezin'!"

"What's your name?" Kyle said, his dimples deepening, his blond hair catching the sun. Bryan glared at him. Kyle just blurted it out, asking her name. Why didn't he just go ahead and tell her that he was the popular class clown, and that he and Bryan were the best on their hockey team? Kyle wasn't exactly Mr. Bashful.

"Chelsie," she said, climbing the ladder, goosebumps rising on her arms. "Chelsie Retting." She waved the camera away. "Don't."

Bryan looked from the girl to Kyle, who held the video camera on his shoulder, still filming. Bryan's tongue was a thick ball of cotton.

"I'm Kyle and this is . . ."

Suddenly, swearing bulleted the air.

Bryan spun toward shore. A tangle of teenagers rolled toward them down the dock, cursing, fists swinging.

"Stupid rat!" one kid in jeans shouted. "Why don't you just go home?"

Chelsie stood on the dock. "Oh no!" She wrapped her

19

arms around her waist as though she were suddenly ill.

A boy not much older than Bryan, wearing blue swim trunks and white sneakers, fell out of the circle onto his elbow. Laughter pelleted the air. The boy scrambled to his feet and flailed at the other boys with his arms. His punches looked pathetic.

Grabbing the boy by the wrists and ankles, two teenagers lifted him off the dock.

"Let . . . me . . . go!" the boy shouted, twisting.

The lifeguard blew her shrill whistle.

The teenagers ran awkwardly with the boy down the dock, nearly bowling Bryan over, and began swinging him back and forth over the edge. "One, two . . ."

"I . . . can't . . . swim!"

"Let him go!" Chelsie yelled. "He can't swim!"

"Yeah, right!" one of the teenagers said. "Three!"

Flying through the air, the boy flipped and smacked the water with his stomach, then disappeared below the surface like a skipping-stone.

The lifeguard's whistle shrieked three times.

Howling, the teenage boys took off down the dock.

Bryan glanced from the water to the lifeguard. She was hurrying down her platform ladder. Almost everybody in Minnesota knew how to swim. That kid was old enough to know how. She was wasting her time.

"Where is he?" Kyle said.

Bryan scanned the dark, rippling water. "Uh, I don't know."

Gasping, the boy shot up for air, sputtering and wheezing. "Hel . . ." he choked out, thrashing like an injured bird. He dipped below the surface again.

At the shore end of the dock, one of the boys, taunting,

blocked the lifeguard's path. "Hey, Leah, wannna go out Friday?"

"Out of my way!" she yelled.

Bryan looked back worriedly where the boy had gone under. It would be risky to jump in to rescue someone. He'd be putting his own life in danger. But if he waited much longer, the lifeguard might not be able to find the boy in water nearly as dark as root beer. He watched the rippled surface. The kid was gone.

Bryan's heart beat harder.

"Somebody help him!" Chelsie screamed. "Where is he?"

Bryan scanned the water, the edge of the dock, the shore. Wasn't the kid going to surface again? He'd disappeared so fast! Bryan couldn't just stand back and watch.

He plunged in.

CHAPTER FOUR

Bryan swam to the spot where the boy had last surfaced. Was this a joke? Had the kid swum away underwater? He hesitated, treading water. He didn't want to be the butt of someone's prank.

He looked down into the darkness and spotted something white below the surface. With a gulp of air, he dove below.

In the cold darkness, he opened his eyes and groped at the white shape. He touched it—a shoe, then an ankle. He grabbed hold and reversed his position, dragging the boy up and up. Harder. Pull harder. His lungs ached, burned, ready to burst.

Bryan broke the surface. He drank in air.

"C'mon!" Kyle shouted.

The lifeguard stretched out a long hooked pole. With one hand, Bryan grabbed the pole, with the other, he held fast to the boy's ankle.

The lifeguard leaned over and pulled the boy's limp body closer to the dock. Kyle and Chelsie helped lift him up.

Shaking, Bryan swam a few strokes to the ladder, grabbed it, and climbed. He hurried over to the boy.

The lifeguard was kneeling. "He must have choked down water," she said. She rolled the boy on his side, letting water spill from his mouth. Then she pushed him onto his back, tilted his head, and poised her lips above his open mouth. She inhaled, then blew, her mouth firmly sealed against his and one hand under the boy's chin.

Bryan was glad she had made it in time for this part. He didn't want to give mouth-to-mouth—not to a boy, anyway.

The boy started coughing, like a car engine sputtering reluctantly on a frozen morning, and pushed away from the lifeguard. He rose to his hands and knees, slowly crawled two feet away, and threw up over the edge of the dock. His body was ghostly white.

"Bry," Kyle said, patting Bryan on the back. "He might have died if it wasn't for you!"

"Yeah, good job!" exclaimed a man in red trunks, part of a gathering crowd.

"Thanks," the lifeguard said to Bryan. "They blocked me. I couldn't get . . ." She stopped and bit down on her trembling lip.

Bryan was stunned. One minute, the boy was in the middle of a fight on the dock, the next he was in the water, drowning. One minute, Bryan was stumbling over how to speak to a girl, the next thing he knew he was a hero.

The boy stood, wobbled, then doubled over again, his knobby spine protruding.

Chelsie put her hand reassuringly on the boy's heaving back. "You're gonna be okay, Cam. You're gonna be okay." With her other hand, she reached over and grabbed Bryan's wrist.

"Thanks for savin' my brother," she said. Her hand was

23

warm. "I froze. I hate myself." She squeezed her eyes shut, then opened them and let out her breath. "I didn't know what to do. . . ."

She looked away and removed her hand from Bryan's arm.

"Your brother?" Bryan could still feel the warmth of her fingers against his wet skin.

Chelsie nodded.

"Somebody call the newspaper," a lady in pink shorts and top said. "That boy should have his picture in the paper." She pointed at Bryan. "He's a hero!"

"Wait," someone else called out. "I saw Nancy Benton on the beach. Maybe she has her camera with her."

Picture in the paper? A hero for rescuing a rat? Wouldn't Dad love that! No, better to slip away quietly. He hadn't meant to get in the middle of anything. But Bryan couldn't move.

Kyle looked at him and frowned. "Bry? Are you feeling all right? You look awful."

Bryan let out a ragged breath and gazed across the lake at the silhouetted pine trees. He wished he could skip the country and disappear into Canada, which lay on the opposite shore.

"Yeah, I'm okay, I just . . ."

A woman in a sleek brown swimsuit tapped him on the shoulder. "I got it all with my zoom lens from shore," she said, extending her hand.

Bryan looked at her hand, dumbly, then realized she was talking to him. He shook it gingerly.

"I'm Nancy Benton with the *Daily News*. May I ask a few questions?" She flipped open a notepad and clicked her pen. "And to think I was going to take today off . . . happens every time," she said to herself. "So . . . what happened here?" she said.

Bryan glanced toward the shore. The three teenagers were gone. He hesitated. "Uh," he began. "I'm not sure. I didn't really see what happened." He couldn't tell her what had happened, not if it was going to be in the newspaper. Besides, he didn't know who the teenagers were. He wasn't lying, not really—just not telling the whole truth. "I was diving, and when I got out, I saw this boy in the water . . . crying for help."

"What made you dive in after him?"

Bryan shrugged. He looked over at Chelsie, who was wrapping a faded yellow towel around her brother's thin shoulders. "I don't know," he answered. "Can I go now?"

"Just a few more quick questions . . ."

After the interview, Bryan spotted Chelsie sitting on the edge of the dock, shoulder to shoulder with her brother. She was dangling her feet in the water, her head down. Cam was bundled in a towel, shaking.

"Wait up," Bryan whispered to Kyle. He walked up behind her. Water dripped from her ponytail down the peachy skin of her back.

"Is he going to be okay?" Bryan asked.

Chelsie flinched, then looked up, her eyes wide. "Oh good, it's you." She nodded. "Yeah, I think he'll be fine."

Bryan hesitated, his feet turning to lead weights. He didn't move his arms. He certainly couldn't look her in the eyes. "I'm sorry it happened."

"They . . . hate . . . us," said Cam, without raising his head.

Chelsie lifted her chin and forced a smile at Bryan. "It wasn't your fault. I guess some folks have a strange sense of humor, that's all." She crossed her arms over her chest.

"Well . . ." Bryan said, and glanced from Chelsie toward Kyle. "Well . . ."

"That's a deep subject," said Kyle.

Bryan rolled his eyes. He'd kill Kyle later. "Umm . . . I better go."

Bryan and Kyle walked across the beach and grabbed their bikes from the rack.

"Why'd they throw him in, anyway?" Kyle asked. "Just because he's a 'rat'?"

Bryan leaned down and unsnapped his black plastic water bottle from his bike. He took a long drink. "I don't know. Adults who work for Badgett are rats, but I don't know about their kids."

Halfway to town, as they biked side by side over a bridge-covered stream, Bryan's eyes began to burn. He rubbed them with the back of his hand. He tried not to breathe. A ripe stench hung in the air.

The mill's dumping ground had been the source of editorial complaints all summer from people who lived near it. They complained of not being able to sleep at night, of coughing and getting sick to their stomachs, of not being able to sell their houses. Why hadn't Bryan noticed this smell on his way to the beach? Maybe the wind had shifted.

"That's what money smells like," Bryan said.

"Yeah," said Kyle, scrunching his nose and pedaling faster. "It stinks!"

Leaning his bike against the inside wall of his garage, Bryan stepped toward the door leading to the kitchen. He heard the raised voices of his parents. The whole summer, it seemed his parents did nothing but fight. It hadn't always been that way. He turned the handle slowly and walked inside.

Still in her workout suit, Mom squared her hands on her hips. Even the twins knew not to mess with her when she stood like that. "Is it really worth it—all this tension over jobs?"

Bryan took off his Nike tennis shoes and lined them up neatly next to Dad's. They were nearly the same size. He pretended not to hear his parents' argument.

"Worth it? Worth it?!" Dad shouted, his face dark with anger. He slammed his fist down on the counter, something Bryan had never seen him do before.

Bryan pressed his back against the corner counter, hoping to escape notice.

"You want me to work as an electrician on the road," Dad asked, "leaving home for a month or two at a time? Is that what you want? Tell me, what kind of life is that?"

As much as Bryan hated their fighting, he couldn't move. He wanted to know what was going on around town, too. If his world was going to unravel, he at least wanted to know when it was going to happen.

"It's union bashing!" Dad continued loudly. A deep shade of red climbed from above his T-shirt collar. "That's what Gold Portage's up to. If guys like me aren't willing to stand up, then pretty soon all us locals will be locked right out of here."

When Dad had first used the phrase "locked out," Bryan had stupidly pictured a fence going up around the whole town, locking out all union workers. But Dad had explained it meant not getting the work, not getting a chance at it because it was already given to a nonunion-hiring construction company.

"Pretty soon it will spread beyond this expansion

project to the paper mill itself, and everybody will be working for peanuts! The biggest, multimillion-dollar project in Minnesota, and we're not getting a piece of it! We're not going to let them take away our jobs without putting up a fight. This is a battle, one that big business and unions all across America are keeping their eyes on! If we don't take a stand . . ."

"Dad?" Bryan asked, his voice a squeak next to Dad's baritone.

Dad ignored him.

"You think I could have built this house on peanuts?!" Dad demanded, his arms stretched wide.

"I'm working now, too, remember?" Mom said.

A sharp smell filled the air. Smoke curled from the edges of the oven door and swirled upward.

Mom spun toward the oven. "Oh, shoot!"

Bryan grabbed hot pads from the drawer behind him and yanked the pan from the oven. What should have been broiled salmon steaks looked more like slabs of black moon rock.

"All this tension—I can't even concentrate anymore!" Mom wailed as she opened the door to the garage. Bryan carried out the sizzling pan and set it on Dad's tool bench.

"Thanks, Bry," Mom said. "I'm glad *you* know how to keep your head when some of us are losing ours." She glared at Dad.

"Yeah, well, maybe," Dad said, "Bryan and everybody else around here needs to lift their heads out of the sand!"

Mom raised her hands like a traffic cop. "Enough, Stan," she said. "Enough! Dinner's already ruined. Let's drop the whole labor dispute and go out to eat like we used to, okay? Let's try to have a nice evening for a change." She paused, letting out a deep breath, then touched Dad's elbow. "Please?"

Dad shrugged. His anger was already subsiding.

"I'll get the twins," she said. She turned away and headed out the sliding screen door.

"Dad," Bryan whispered, stepping closer. "I don't want you to work out of town either." Bryan didn't like it when Dad took one- and two-month jobs away from home. When Dad was gone, home was a blanket with a giant hole cut out of its center. "I want to help," he said.

"Thanks." Dad reached over and tousled Bryan's hair. "I'm sorry I'm taking it out on the family. It's just that . . . ah, I don't know." He walked to the kitchen window and gazed out. With his back to Bryan, he slowly rubbed the back of his neck. He seemed to have forgotten Bryan was there. Under his breath he said, "Tonight we'll show 'em."

Tonight.

The word stuck in Bryan's mind. He couldn't get it out of his mind all through dinner at Jim's Cafe, or when he snuck downstairs to watch the tape, replaying Chelsie's back dive over and over. He couldn't help thinking about it as he fell asleep on his top bunk. What was Dad going to do tonight?

CHAPTER FIVE

Bryan forced his eyes open in the darkness and lifted his watch from the shelf behind his head. The numbers glowed in the dark: 2:20. He'd heard something. Below, Josh's slow breathing came in soft waves. Maybe he'd imagined it.

Click. The kitchen door leading to the garage opened and closed softly.

Easing back the covers, Bryan swung his legs over the sideboard and searched for the steps of the ladder. When he gained secure footing, he climbed down, careful not to wake Josh. He pulled on his jeans and hooded sweatshirt, then slipped out to the empty kitchen. Slowly, he turned the handle to the garage, stepped into the smell of oil and stacked wood, and closed the door silently behind him. He crouched by the minivan and didn't move.

Dad was pushing against the front of his pickup, inching the truck silently out of the garage. Bryan almost called out, but stopped himself. He ducked down and peered through the windows of the van. Clearly, Dad didn't want the family to know what he was doing. When the truck was halfway out, Dad hurried to the driver's seat and jumped in.

Bryan shuffled quietly toward the van's tailpipe and

watched from the edge of the open garage door.

PROUD TO BE AMERICAN, PROUD TO BE UNION, read a sticker on the front bumper. The truck rolled backward down the sloping driveway to the road. What in the world? It was strange to watch Dad sneaking around. Something about it made the hair on the back of Bryan's neck bristle.

On the street, the truck rolled to a stop. Dad jumped out and began pushing the truck from behind.

Bryan had to know what was going on. He grabbed his ten-speed from the corner, swung his leg over the center bar, and hid in the shadows. A cricket chirped, its song echoing in the still air.

Gliding out slowly on his bike, Bryan stopped behind the lilac bushes. Yesterday Dad had told him that the lilacs had already set their buds for spring. In the buds, everything they would become was already predetermined. Lavender lilacs again, no choice about it. And Bryan had thought it was pretty much the same way with people. Bryan and his dad were so much alike. He was his father's son, for better or for worse.

When the truck had rolled about twenty feet beyond the driveway, the engine rumbled into gear.

Bryan biked down the freshly mowed lawn, past the silver mailbox, and followed at a distance. Cool night air rushed through his hair and against his face, slapping him fully awake.

The truck moved slowly through the neighborhood of new, large houses, past the Grinkos', Sheenans', and Kalowskis'. A small light glimmered at Kyle's house, but Bryan knew from overnights there that the Kalowskis always kept a light on.

The truck rumbled so loudly that Bryan was sure all of

Cedar Ridge Addition would wake up. He held his breath and watched the houses. What if someone saw them? Wouldn't they think it looked strange? Would they call the police?

Bryan swallowed hard. And what would Dad do if he saw him in the rearview mirror? He tried to hang back, to not get too close. The truck moved slowly enough for Bryan to keep up. He waited for his dad to turn on the lights, but the truck remained a dark shadow.

Then it began to move faster. Bryan pedaled harder. He shivered—partly from the chilly, early September air, but mostly from excitement. For the first time in a long while, he felt like he was part of what his dad was doing. Not the same closeness they had on their fishing trips—which, until this summer, had happened every free weekend—but still something important. Bryan was pretty sure it had to do with the rats.

The truck wound through backstreets, avoiding the city's well-lit main streets. At an approaching intersection, a white police car with two officers inside crossed and headed north. If they noticed Dad's truck without lights, they'd stop him. Bryan held his breath. The police car moved on.

Bryan followed the truck through the intersection, careful to lag farther behind under the lights. He pumped his legs hard to catch up again and, three blocks farther, followed the truck down an alley. The truck slowed, then pulled up behind a small house with a white picket fence. The motor cut.

Bryan skidded to a stop behind a wide spruce tree, only ten yards away. Whose house was this? He glanced around, hoping some mad watchdog wasn't going to pounce on his leg. He waited, the sound of his own breathing and heart-beat cranked to full volume.

Dad sat in the truck, not moving.

The door of a small house opened. In the shadows, a bulky, short man glanced up and down the alley, then lumbered toward the truck. It was the man with caterpillar eyebrows.

Dad climbed out, stepped to the back of the truck, and lifted his toolbox onto the edge. He opened the lid and pulled out a mallet.

He lifted up a brown bag, too. Suddenly the sound of metal against metal filled the air. He dropped it.

"Shoot. The bottom of the bag got wet."

He huffed, looked around, then waved his hand at the man. They disappeared down the alley.

Bryan waited a few seconds, then put down his kick-stand, and inched toward the truck. From the open rear window came the smell of worn vinyl and sweat. Bryan reached into the bed of the pickup. Something sharp pricked his finger. Again he reached, more carefully. This time, he picked up a handful of long, sharp tacks. He'd heard about tacks being tossed in the streets over the summer. So this is what Dad had dropped. He scooped three handfuls of tacks onto the torn paper bag, gathered the paper edges together and twisted it closed, like a big Hershey's Kiss. Then he slipped quietly down the alley after his father.

When he reached the corner, he spotted two silhouettes halfway down the block. Quickly he walked toward them, his footsteps muffled in the damp grass along the sidewalks.

This neighborhood had some of the rattier houses in town. Then he caught his own joke. Rattier. *Rats.* Though most of the workers lived at the housing camp southwest of his neighborhood, he'd heard that workers with families rented here. Unlike his neighborhood—where new two-story houses, complete with decks and two-stall garages, sprouted up as quickly as dandelions after a rain—the houses here were small and old. To his right, a shutter hung limply on broken hinges. The lower entry step was broken. A tire filled with flowers decorated the overgrown lawn. Maybe this was all rats could afford to live in. Is this what it meant to work for Badgett—to live on a lot less money? If unions helped people to earn better wages so they could live better, then unions were a good thing.

He heard his dad's low whisper, which never was very quiet, even at church, but he couldn't hear what he was saying. The two men moved between cars parked on the west side of the street. What were they doing?

His father, a dark shadow, squatted next to the rear tire of a dark-colored station wagon.

Pfffft. It was a squeaky puff of air. Dad moved to the front tire. *Pfffft.* Bryan's stomach turned. He suddenly understood. Dad was slitting the car's tires.

Tonight. So this was what Dad meant.

Kyle had said his dad's insurance office was overloaded with claims this summer from vandalism, and Bryan had told him that rats were probably responsible. He stared at his dad's shadow, bent over. Was this any different than tossing stones at the guardhouse? Probably not. It was simply proving a point. It was voicing an opinion.

If Dad saw him on the curb, just standing by, watching, he'd be mad. It was time to act. Either turn around and head home, or help.

Hand shaking, Bryan untwisted the wad of paper and grabbed a handful of one-inch tacks. Their sharp points

34

pricked his palm. *"He's a hero!"* The words pierced his conscience, sharper than the tacks. He looked around the street at the small houses. He didn't know anyone who lived here—their names, their children's names. For all he knew, Chelsie and her brother could live in this neighborhood. His body twitched. He took two slow steps backwards, then turned. The tacks fell from his hand, back into the paper.

A shattering of glass broke the night air. *Ca-crash!*

Bryan jumped, his heart pounding. He dropped the paper pouch and tacks spilled all around him.

He watched as the short man moved away from a sports car, its window caved in. With the mallet raised high, the man ran to the next car, slammed the mallet into the windshield, and took off.

"Let's go!" he whispered hoarsely to Bryan's father. The two men raced toward Bryan.

Bryan froze, only yards away.

Dad spotted him. "What?!"

Picking a path through the tacks, he ran to his dad. "I tossed those tacks," he lied.

"Oh no," Dad groaned, shaking his head. "This isn't for kids, Bry. Follow me!"

Somewhere behind them, a door slammed open.

A man swore. Bang!! A single shot of gunfire rang out in the black night and set off a chorus of barking dogs.

Bryan tore down the street alongside his dad, the short man at their heels. His heartbeat thundered in his ears like a kettledrum. They raced down the alley and threw Bryan's bike into the pickup. Maybe this wasn't for kids, but Bryan was in deep now.

Then they sped away, headlights off.

CHAPTER SIX

With night dew still clinging to his skin, Bryan climbed back under his quilt, chilled. He fell into a fitful sleep, dreaming once of getting caught with a mallet in his hand and once of standing next to Chelsie in the grocery store—of all places—leaning forward to actually kiss her, his lips just about to touch hers, but then her face turning into a wet nose and a hairy snout. Gretsky. Gross!

"C'mon sleepy," came Mom's voice from next to his bunk. She pushed Bryan's hair away from his forehead. "Time to get up."

"What . . . what time is it?" he asked groggily, his mouth rancid as old potatoes.

"Nearly eleven o'clock. You know how fidgety Grandma Effie gets if we're late. She said noon, but she's sure to be pacing by now."

From his great-grandparents' compact living room, Bryan could see Elissa and Josh sitting at the glass-topped kitchen table, drinking milk and eating cookies. Being older had its privileges; at least Bryan could eat in the living room. As the adults drank coffee, he dunked another sugar-sprinkled gingersnap in his glass of milk, let it soak for three seconds, then popped it in his mouth.

With grandparents in Arizona and St. Cloud, Bryan actually felt closest to Grandma Effie and Grandpa Howie, his great-grandparents. He could visit them anytime he wanted to.

"The strike of 1934," Grandpa Howie said slowly, the words taking shape on his dry, wrinkled lips, "was part of Teamster history."

"It was something," Grandma Effie said. "We lived in Minneapolis then. Stan was just born—youngest of five." Her mind was still as quick as her fingers darting the needle in and out of the quilting frame on her lap. "I was down there in the soup kitchens, keeping those men fed day and night, day and night, keeping their spirits up. Oh, and it was a long strike. Not like today. Things are easy today. Then," she said, pausing to rethread her needle, "men were fighting to earn enough money to feed their families. Some starved right in the streets."

"When things got bad," Grandpa added, "it was hand-to-hand combat." He swung his left arm to demonstrate. His right arm, which years ago had gotten tangled in a paper machine, was a stub at the elbow beneath his pinned shirt-sleeve. After Grandpa's accident, the union had pushed for safer working conditions. "If we weren't fighting the police and their billy clubs, then . . ."

Grandma jumped in. "And it was bloody, they . . ."

"Let me finish," Grandpa ordered. "If we weren't fighting the police, then it was the Citizen's Party. And they were folks, mostly in business, who had it in their heads that forming a union meant joining the Communist Party."

"Did it?" Bryan asked.

37

"Heck no!" Grandpa said. "But there were plenty of Reds around then . . ."

Bryan glanced at Mom. She was staring past Grandpa, her fist pressed against her lips. Usually, she reacted to the word *reds*—slang for "communists," but this time it went right past her. Bryan couldn't see why it mattered anyway. It was only a word.

Grandpa continued, " . . . especially in Minnesota, so people were nervous. We were fighting for our families, for our jobs. We worked twelve-to-sixteen-hour days, six days a week, and still we couldn't support our families. What kind of a life was that? Not much of one, I'll tell you that!" He leaned forward on his cane, his eyes half closed.

Bryan sat on Grandma's gold easy chair. He wished they were at an outside picnic on Labor Day, instead of inside visiting. The windows were closed, locking in stale air. No matter what time of year, Grandma was always afraid of getting chilled and catching pneumonia.

Bryan yawned.

Grandpa turned to Dad. "So Stan, how goes the war? What are you guys doing to make sure the paper mill hears you?"

"We're out there with picket signs," Dad said. He looked Grandpa in the eyes. "We're shaking things up and not letting them forget about us."

Mom looked at Dad and crossed her arms. "It's too much shaking up, if you ask me. People are going to get hurt if this town doesn't settle down. Personally," she said in a level voice, "I've had enough, thank you."

Bryan looked at his parents' stern faces. The tension was thick as wet cement. A pain jabbed him. He knew of plenty of kids whose parents had divorced. Could this strike

38

break up his parents? He sure hoped not.

Dad's eyes met Bryan's. He nodded slightly, as if to warn Bryan to not mention a word about last night.

Bryan nodded back and forced a slight smile.

Grandpa leaned forward onto his knees and picked up his cane. He pounded it on the floor. "Stan, you got to get mad! You've never really known what it means to put up a fight."

Dad moved his lips, as though ready to speak, then stopped. He stood up and paced in front of the three-tiered plant stand by the window. "Grandpa," he said, smoothing the air with the flat of his hand, "we've got it under control. Trust me."

"Under control?" The spider veins in Grandpa's face grew redder. "You got to get mad and fight!"

"I disagree," Mom said. She carefully folded her hands over her crossed knees.

Grandpa glared at her, as though she didn't have the right to disagree.

"That's the exact attitude I try to correct in my first graders," Mom continued. "If people always have to fight to solve problems, then what kind of a world is it? Sure, I want Stan to be able to work here. But if things don't go his way, we'll get by somehow. If we have to move, then we'll move." Her fingers were laced together, her knuckles turning white.

"I don't want to move," Bryan joined, tapping his right heel nervously on the carpet. "Where else could I get on such a good hockey team? Besides, we're going to have a great peewee season, but we can't do it without Dad."

He hadn't meant to get involved in the conversation, but it slipped out. Maybe he was getting older after all. He sat up straighter.

Dad gave him a wink, as if he'd just scored a goal.

Grandma Effie cleared her throat. "Well, it's different in some ways. The workers get paid pretty well. Grandpa didn't buy his new pickup without making some pretty good wages over the years at the mill. Things aren't as desperate as back then. No, it's different these days."

"Same thing!" Grandpa said, and pounded his cane down once, then twice. The coffee table vibrated.

"Howard!" said Grandma. "Be careful!"

"I think Grandpa's right," Bryan said, glancing at Dad. Dad had made it clear he didn't want him too involved, but he hadn't forbidden him from speaking. "This strike is no different than Grandpa's strike. We've got to fight for our rights now, just like then. Whatever it takes."

Mom looked sideways at Bryan and Dad, then slowly shook her head.

CHAPTER SEVEN

The next day, after a midmorning breakfast, Bryan combed his hair in the bathroom mirror, brushed his teeth, and put on the deodorant he'd bought for the first time last week. "Mom," he'd said, "I think my pits stink." She'd sent him to Kmart with five dollars to buy his own. He'd picked out a green-and-white brand, same kind as Dad's.

He went to the piano, sat down, and thumbed through the pages of his greatest hits book, looking for a good song to play. The doorbell rang.

"I'll get it!" Elissa said. She jumped up from her game of Chutes and Ladders on the living-room floor with Josh. They were both still in pajamas. Elissa bounded for the door.

"No!" Josh said, scrambling to his feet. "I'll get it!"

"I called it first!" Elissa screamed, tugging at the back of Josh's jet-patterned pajama bottoms.

Josh pulled at the handle and fell back on top of Elissa. They tumbled in a heap. Elissa started crying and slugged Josh in the side.

Mom's voice came from the basement. "What's going

on up there?"

In the open doorway stood Chelsie, in a cream sweater, the morning light softly blanketing her shoulders. Behind her was Cam.

"Hi," said Chelsie. She was holding a white box with a red bow.

Bryan swung his legs over the piano bench, his face growing hot. She was at *his* door with a gift? This was too much. Wait until Kyle heard about this.

"Uh, hi," he said casually, stepping toward the door. He jammed his hands in his jean pockets. "What's up?"

"Here. This is for you."

Bryan's mom came up the stairs. "Who's here? Oh, hi."

"Mom," Bryan said, "uh . . . this is Chelsie and her brother, um . . ."

"Cam," Chelsie said, glancing at Cam. She flipped her french braid over her shoulder.

"Yeah, Cam. I met them at the beach yesterday."

Chelsie smiled, but Cam's expression didn't change. It was blank, impossible to read.

"From our mom and dad . . ." Cam said slowly, as if he'd rehearsed the words, ". . . for savin' . . . my life." His voice was slow and a bit mechanical.

Mom looked hard at Bryan. "Saving your life? What's this? I haven't heard a word." She looked back at Chelsie. "Tell me . . . Oh, I'm sorry. We're making you stand there in the door. Come in," she said, waving her arms toward the kitchen. "Are you kids too old for a Popsicle?"

Bryan rolled his eyes. If Mom did *anything*, anything at all to embarrass him now, he'd die.

"Sounds great," Chelsie said.

Cam shook his head.

"I want grape!" said Elissa.

"Me, too," said Josh.

Before Mom could open the freezer door, Josh beat her to it and grabbed the Popsicle box. "Last grape," he said, grinning at Elissa.

Bryan held his breath. He knew this meant war. Couldn't Josh and Elissa act civilized for once? He glanced over at Chelsie, who was holding back a smile. When her eyes caught his, he quickly looked away.

"That's not fair!" Elissa said, her lower lip protruding farther with each second.

Mom pushed both palms forward. "Stop it," she said. "You two go to your rooms for forgetting your manners. The grape Popsicle goes back in the freezer. Neither of you gets it."

Josh stared at Mom hard and shook his blond head slightly.

"Go," Mom said. "I'm not joking."

Shoulders sagging, the twins headed down the hallway, whispering to each other. "It's your fault."

"No, it's your fault."

"I got there first."

Bryan didn't know what to do with himself. He didn't know this girl or her brother. What was he going to talk about? Did they really want to sit in the kitchen with his mom, each eating a Popsicle?

"Let's go out to the deck," Mom said. "I want to hear this story about my heroic son."

After Chelsie and Cam chose their flavors, Bryan picked out a banana Popsicle. He sat in a white deck chair, between Cam and Chelsie.

Gretsky trotted from the backyard and sat at Chelsie's feet. He licked her bare knee, rested his head on her denim shorts, and looked up at her.

"Gretsky," said Bryan, "maybe she doesn't like dogs."

"I love 'em!" Chelsie said. She pushed her face closer to Gretsky's. "I've always wanted one, but my dad said it wouldn't be fair to the dog on account of our movin' so much. I don't think it's fair to *me*."

Chelsie scratched under Gretsky's red collar; Gretsky leaned into her fingers and groaned contentedly. "He's so adorable."

Lucky dog, Bryan thought.

Chelsie handed the gift to Bryan.

"Okay," Mom said. "I know it's not Bryan's birthday, so what's this all about?"

"Open it," said Chelsie. Cam's dark eyes smiled.

Bryan hesitated, then pulled off the red bow and opened the small white box. Inside, beneath a lining of wax paper, were chocolate candies. This was too much. He was getting chocolates from Chelsie? Well, not really from her—from her parents, her family.

Cam spoke up. "I fell off . . . the dock," he said. "And . . . I don't . . . swim very good."

"That's for sure," Chelsie said, glancing at Cam. "I learned to swim when I was really young, but Cam never liked the water. Then we were movin' around so much— every year or so—that he never learned."

The smile in Cam's eyes faded. His stony expression returned.

"So," Mom said, circling her hand for more details.

"Everybody just stood around," said Chelsie. "I froze up. I didn't know what to do—but Bryan dove right in after him."

44

Mom leaned forward on her knees. "Yes?"

"He dove underwater," Chelsie said excitedly, "and came right back to the surface with him. I don't know how he did it, because I couldn't see anything! I thought the water would be crystal clear here, but it's so dark."

"It's minerals," Bryan said. He felt the need to defend the water, as if he didn't have enough battles lately. "Really, the water's clean."

"Wasn't there a lifeguard there?" Mom asked, looking at Bryan.

"She was there," Bryan began, "but she wasn't coming fast enough."

"Guess that makes you a hero," she said, playing with the opal necklace Dad had given her last Valentine's Day. "That's you, Bry. You're a doer, not just a talker."

Bryan didn't respond. He didn't like all the attention drawn to himself.

"When you were little, you used to run outside after a rain and rescue earthworms from robins."

Right. Mom made him sound like a knight in shining armor. He felt more like a slug and wished he could slither away. He glanced at his right knee, which was pumping up and down a hundred beats per second, and stopped himself.

"Are your parents here with the construction project?" Mom asked.

How could she? How could she come right out and ask it?

Chelsie and Cam both nodded. Neither spoke.

Bryan's stomach muscles contracted. He pressed his thumb against his jaw and stroked his upper lip with his forefinger.

45

"Have you had any trouble?" Mom asked. "How are people around here treating you?"

Chelsie shrugged. "I don't know."

Cam's face didn't move.

"You didn't just fall off the dock, then," Mom said to Cam. It wasn't a question, more of a stated fact. She should have been an attorney.

Cam shook his head of dark hair. "Thrown in . . . some guys . . . were calling . . . me a rat."

Bryan wondered how the teenagers knew Cam was a . . . was from out of town. A number of the out-of-town workers were Hispanic, their skin much darker than Cam's. At stores, Bryan heard some people using faltering English. It made them moving targets in a nearly all-white community. Then again, in a small town, just being new was enough to make a person stand out.

"My folks would have driven over here to thank you themselves," Chelsie said, "but this mornin' they drove over some tacks on our street."

Bryan froze.

"And someone slit the tires on the neighbor's car and bashed in their windshield." Her smile had vanished. She looked blankly at Bryan's mom. "Why would someone do that?" she asked in a pained whisper.

Bryan's tongue turned leathery. His stomach felt queasy. When he looked down at his hands, he saw they were trembling. He eased them under his thighs to keep them still, to hide them.

"Oh, I'm sorry to hear that," Mom said. She shook her head back and forth. "I'm so sorry."

Bryan stared at the straight boards of the deck. A fire had started underneath him and he was being roasted from his feet up. His chest grew hotter and hotter; then his neck, chin, ears, and forehead burned. Could they tell how much he was holding back? Could they read his mind about what he'd done? It wasn't against them, really. He wouldn't have done anything to hurt them.

"Where do you live, anyway?" Bryan asked, glancing up quickly.

Chelsie's eyes met his, held him for a moment, then let him go. He looked down at the ground, trying to act casual, as if her answer didn't really matter.

"Three thirty-seven Hastings Street. South end of town."

"Oh," Bryan answered hastily, "I was just wondering." He and his dad were on Hastings Street. His head spun. How could he have known it was their street?

The phone rang in the house. Mom jumped up to get it.

Bryan had to get a grip on himself. He picked up the white box and held it out to Cam and Chelsie. "Here, have some. And thank your parents for me, okay?"

"Bryan," Chelsie began, reaching for the box and taking out a chocolate. Her eyes reminded him of a wounded animal. "Do you have any idea who might have . . ."

Mom slid open the sliding screen door before she could finish. "Carl Hunter called for you, Bryan."

"The sheriff?"

"He wants you to come down to his office."

Bryan tried to swallow. His face tingled. Had someone seen him?

"Hey, you can relax," Mom said, her voice tight. "It's me you have to worry about, Bry, not the police. You left the video camera at the beach."

"Oh," Bryan said, relieved. He let out a silent breath.

47

Mom continued. "I made myself very clear about taking care of that camera. Lucky for you, someone was nice enough to turn it in to the sheriff's office. Otherwise you *would* be in deep trouble." She looked at Chelsie and Cam, then turned to Bryan. "He said you can pick it up anytime."

Bryan jumped up. He couldn't sit there a minute longer and keep up this act. Getting the camera gave him the excuse he needed. "I'll go get it."

Chelsie and Cam stood up and followed Bryan into the house.

"We better go," Chelsie said. Stepping out the front door, she turned to Bryan. "You know, you're a good diver."

"What?" He blinked. Her compliment caught him off guard. Then he realized she'd probably only seen his flop. "Oh, a joke," he said and tried to laugh. "I get it."

"No." She shook her head. "I watched your dives from the beach. I meant it."

Why couldn't he even make small talk?

"Well, you're not too bad yourself," he said, sounding like a bad movie script. He shoved his hands in his pockets. "See ya."

He closed the front door, leaned against it, and let out a long, heavy breath. Chelsie's skin, her voice—everything about her—seemed soft. Her unfinished question burrowed deep under his skin. He felt like a chicken, a liar, a hypocrite.

Do you have any idea who . . . ?

CHAPTER EIGHT

Bryan entered the Koochiching County Law Enforcement Building and, at the front desk, asked about his camera. An officer with a toothpick between his teeth led him down the hall to a door marked SHERIFF CARL HUNTER.

The sheriff leaned forward in his chair, stretched out his hand in a solid handshake, and nodded toward one of the chairs. He moved his Hardee's bag off to the side. The sheriff's eyes were as many shades of blue as a June sky. His face looked as pliable as worn leather, changing quickly from a scowl into a smile.

"Just finishing lunch. Have a seat, Bryan."

"Thanks." Bryan sat in the wooden chair.

Carl Hunter's pale green office was a clutter of papers, manuals, newspapers, and coffee cups. It smelled stale. On the front of his desk was a large red and white NO SMOKING sign. Behind his desk hung a print of a dozen mallards taking off in a marshy bay. "So, how's it going?" the sheriff asked, his voice warm.

"Uh, fine," Bryan said. He leaned back, but decided that that looked too relaxed, like he had an attitude problem.

49

He leaned forward. He sat up straight and tried to keep from fidgeting.

The sheriff spun his chair around and reached on top of the gray file cabinet for the black video camera. With both hands, he picked it up, spun back toward Bryan and set the camera in the center of his desk, keeping his hands on it. "Is this yours?"

"Yeah," Bryan said. Was there something wrong with the video camera? Did he think Bryan stole it or something? "I forgot it, I guess, at the beach yesterday."

"I hear you made yourself into a hero, too," Sheriff Hunter said, his big hands still glued to the camera. "Saved a kid from drowning, isn't that so?"

Bryan shifted in his chair. "It was no big deal. He went under and . . . the lifeguard wasn't coming fast enough. Somebody had to help him."

"I'm proud of you, Bryan," the sheriff said. "Our community could use more young people like you." He paused.

The sheriff was drawing out the conversation longer than necessary, searching for something more.

Bryan glanced down. He was tugging at the seam on the sides of his jeans. He pushed his hands under his thighs and sat on them.

Sheriff Hunter let go of the video camera. He grabbed a pencil from a cup that said IT'S THE LAW and turned it slowly between his fingers. The large gold ring on the sheriff's left hand caught the light from the window and pierced Bryan's eyes.

Bryan flinched and looked away.

"There's a lot of trouble brewing around town, Bryan. . . ." He waited. "I'm sure you're aware of some of it. . . ."

Bryan curled his toes inside his sneakers. What was the sheriff searching for? He might as well put him under bright investigation lights! Did he know about last night? If so, why not just say it?

"I went to high school with your dad." He paused. "How's he doing these days . . . with the strike and all?" The sheriff leaned forward onto his elbows.

"Well . . ." Bryan looked at the duck print behind the desk. He rubbed his wet palms together and took a deep breath. "He's not too happy with what's going on with the rats—I mean, with Badgett. He doesn't want to have to move out of the area to find work, so he doesn't think it's very fair . . . that's all." He shrugged. "I don't know. Things could be better, I guess."

Sheriff Hunter looked hard at Bryan, blue eyes probing. "Are you a hockey player, too, like your dad?"

Bryan nodded. He didn't want to come right out and say that he always played first string.

The sheriff continued. "He was good—one of the best. What do you play?"

"Center, usually. Sometimes right wing, sometimes left wing." He couldn't take this anymore. He jumped up. "Can I take my video camera now?"

"Sure," said the sheriff. He stood, too, and handed the camera across the desk to Bryan.

Bryan was surprised to see that the sheriff wasn't much taller than he was—maybe five feet seven inches at most. Somehow, Bryan had expected the sheriff to tower over him. He took the camera and tried to sound cheery. "Thanks."

The sheriff walked around the desk and put his hand on Bryan's shoulder. "Just one more thing," he said.

51

Bryan waited, chewing on his inner lip. Footsteps echoed in the hallway. Maybe an officer was bringing someone to the second floor to lock them behind the second-story bars Bryan had seen from outside.

"If you hear about anyone damaging other people's property," said the sheriff, his eyes fixed on Bryan's, "if you catch wind of anyone breaking the law over this labor dispute—do me a favor. Come by and see me, okay?"

Bryan adjusted the strap of his camera over his shoulder and forced a smile. "Sure."

He turned and walked casually down the linoleum hallway past the officers' break room, where two police officers sat with coffee cups. He continued past the service desk at the entrance and walked out the door.

Calmly, he rolled his bike away from the red stone building, lowered the kickstand, and hopped on. The air was heavy with the smell of rain.

One block from the jail, Bryan pushed down hard on the pedals and flew home. The road glistened wet. He welcomed the first drops of water against his face.

CHAPTER NINE

Bryan looked through the new shirts, jeans, and sweatshirts in his closet, deciding what to wear for the first day of school tomorrow. Usually, it mattered. But his conversation with the sheriff still chilled him.

What was Sheriff Hunter getting at? How much did he know? Maybe when the police car had passed through the intersection, the officers had seen Dad's truck and followed them. Maybe they got the license number down. Was the sheriff trying to make him confess?

Bryan heard the truck engine turn off in the garage. The door opened into the kitchen. He heard the murmur of his parents' voices.

"Bry?" Dad called.

Bryan stepped over a pile of Josh's new Lego blocks and walked down the hallway to the kitchen. "Yeah?"

Dad held up the newspaper. "Front page?" he said.

"Isn't that something?" Mom said, pushing her short hair behind her ears. "I'm really proud of him."

Dad needed a shave. He was wet, probably from standing out in the rain on the picket line. He tapped at the black-and-white picture filling up the top quarter of the paper and read the headline HEROIC RESCUE AT CITY BEACH.

Mom smiled. Josh and Elissa raced up the stairs from the basement.

"Dad!" Josh called. "You're home!"

"Dad!" Elissa echoed. "You're home!"

They wrapped their arms around Dad's waist. He set down the paper and squeezed them both around their shoulders.

"Your brother's a hero," Mom said, smiling. She held up the paper.

"Wow!" exclaimed Elissa, shaking her fine blond hair back and forth. She tugged at Bryan's jeans and looked up at him. "I didn't know you were so famous," she added seriously.

"Wait till I tell Alex," Josh said. "He won't believe it."

"It would have to be a rat," Dad said icily.

Bryan winced. "I didn't know him, Dad." He shrugged. "He was just a kid."

"Oh for heaven's sake!" Mom snapped, her eyes fiery. "Josh and Elissa—you two run back downstairs and watch TV. Supper will be ready in a few minutes."

Elissa put out her lip. "But I don't . . ."

"Right now," Mom ordered, placing her hands on the twins' heads. She turned them in the direction of the basement and they trotted down the carpeted stairs.

Mom put her hands on her hips. "Are you serious? A boy was drowning and . . . what do you mean? You think Bryan should have let him drown?" She glared.

"No . . . but he can't be crossing lines!" Dad insisted, his voice sharp.

Bryan cringed. If pulling Cam from the water meant crossing lines, then he was really confused.

With his forefinger, Dad tapped the newspaper lying on the counter. Thump. Thump. Thump. "Stay away from them, Bry. There's trouble brewing—and I don't want you to get hurt."

Mom's face contorted. Tears filled her eyes. "Stan," she said. "Why don't you give me a hand in the kitchen. You and I can talk. It might help to get your mind off the strike for a while."

Dad looked in Mom's direction, but he seemed to be looking right past her. He shook his head.

"Sorry, I can't," he said. "I have to get back."

"But you just got home," she pleaded. "School starts tomorrow. I have a lot to do to get everyone ready."

"Like I said, I better get back." His jaw muscles tightened. He stepped out to the garage and was gone.

Bryan picked up the newspaper lying on the counter and settled onto a stool. In the picture, he was standing by while the lifeguard gave mouth-to-mouth to Cam. The caption read: *Blue Ash youth, Bryan Grant, 12, stands aside after rescuing Cameron Retting, 14, from Rainy Lake Sunday afternoon. Lifeguard Leah Cole revived Retting through mouth-to-mouth resuscitation.* Bryan wondered what Cam thought about the picture—at least the lifeguard was cute. In the background, Chelsie stood with her arms crossed, skin wet, looking on intently. Bryan couldn't take his eyes off her.

After a few minutes, Mom put her hand on Bryan's shoulder. "I don't know your father right now," she said, her voice soft, controlled. Even when she was angry, she had a way of reining in her feelings. "This labor dispute—it's dividing more than union against nonunion." She gripped his shoulder. "It's splitting families like ours right down the middle. I hate it. I absolutely hate it."

She rose, poured two blue glasses full of orange juice, then sat back down. "Here," she said, lifting her glass and passing the other to Bryan. "Bottoms up!"

Bryan lifted the glass to his lips and drained it.

"Mom, when your teacher's union went on strike last year," he said, "it was a lot different, wasn't it?"

Mom sat down beside him on a stool and combed her hair with her fingers. "We didn't have other teachers coming in and taking our positions—that would have made teachers angry. As it was, it just meant closing the classrooms for a few weeks. By striking together, we had more power to get the pay we deserved as professionals."

Bryan understood. He knew his mom worked hard at her job.

Gretsky appeared, sat down next to Bryan's stool, and looked up with his black button nose. Bryan scratched the top of his head.

"Dad's strike is different," she continued. "It's complicated. Rather than walking off a job, they didn't get the job. They're protesting that Gold Portage chose a nonunion contractor to build the new project. It's an unofficial strike, not sanctioned by the union, that's why it's called a wildcat strike."

"Mom," Bryan said, trying to keep his voice casual. "Have you heard about car windows getting bashed in around town, things like that?" He needed to talk about what he knew without coming right out and telling.

She nodded. "Yes, and I hate it. It's one thing to go on strike and wave picket signs. It's another thing entirely to take the law into your own hands and start destroying property, to threaten people." She rested her elbows on the counter. "Just take a look in the paper. There are long columns of vandalism reports every night." She paused.

He remembered the sheriff's stare, the way he seemed to know more than he said. He couldn't meet his mom's eyes.

"Your father doesn't hear a word I say lately. The only people he listens to these days are his buddies at the strike site. I'm afraid he's going to completely stop thinking for himself. He did that once when he was in hockey . . . and it cost him."

Bryan ran his finger around the rim of his empty glass. "What do you mean?"

"His senior year—the year his team went to state—he got so into the competition of it all that he got carried away on the ice. Has he ever mentioned it?"

Bryan shook his head.

"He got into a bad fight in the first period with a player from the other team and had to sit out the rest of the game. His team really needed him. By getting in a fight, he actually hurt his team. He was their best scorer."

"You were a cheerleader at the game?" Bryan asked. He'd seen plenty of Mom's old cheerleading photos; she was always on top of the pyramid.

Mom nodded. "And they lost, six to four," she said. "If your father hadn't been so hotheaded and landed himself in the penalty box, they might have won." She closed her eyes and sighed. "Sometimes he doesn't use any common sense."

What would she say if she knew about the stones Bryan had tossed at the guardhouse or the tacks he'd dropped, even if accidentally? He'd always trusted his parents to know right from wrong, but what happened when they had completely opposite ideas? *Right* wasn't as clear as he'd once thought.

The air was suddenly filled with a putrid smell.

"Mom!" Bryan said.

Her eyes flashed wide. She jumped up to lift the smoking pot from the stove burner. "Not again," she moaned.

Bryan knew the smell all too well. It was the smell of burnt peas permanently bonded to the bottom of a pan.

CHAPTER TEN

By lunch break of the first day of school, Bryan had heard the word "hero" twenty-three times. He swore to himself that the next person who mentioned it, he'd grab by the collar and . . .

"How about a game of kickball?" Kyle said, tossing the black-and-white soccer ball into the air and catching it in both hands. The sky was clear sapphire and breezy. "You and I'll pick teams."

"Sounds good." Bryan looked past the swarm of kids jumping rope, chasing each other, and practicing dance moves next to their tape players. Chelsie stood on the fringe of a cluster of girls near the school doors, the breeze playing with her high ponytail. "Just a second," he said.

He walked over to her.

"Want to play kickball?" he asked. The other three girls stopped talking and huddled closer.

Chelsie looked up at Bryan. If she said no, he'd feel really stupid. She didn't answer right away.

"This isn't a joke, is it?" she asked, sounding angry.

"What? No, I was just wondering if you wanted to play kickball."

Chelsie looked down, then pulled her ponytail across her shoulder and began twisting a few strands of hair into a tight rope. "First," she began, "they said that you said that Cam wasn't really worth saving, because . . . because . . . he was a . . ."

Bryan knew exactly what she was going to say. The word suddenly seemed like a four-letter word. Bryan lowered his voice and stepped closer, his back to the other girls. "Because he's a 'rat,' right?" He studied her face. Chelsie glared at him. "You said it then! I thought you were different."

"No," Bryan said. He shook his head. "No, I didn't say anything like that. It's not true."

Chelsie looked hard at him. "You mean, you *didn't* say it?"

"No." He drew an imaginary X over his chest, but as he did so, he guiltily saw himself spilling tacks into the street. He tried to ignore the picture. He could never tell Chelsie about any of that.

Chelsie waited. "So you don't regret saving Cam?"

"Course not. Is the interrogation over?" he asked. "Can we play kickball now?"

Chelsie nodded. "Sure."

Bryan picked one team; Kyle picked the other. The teams were divided thirteen to twelve, half boys and half girls. Chelsie was Bryan's first pick.

Bryan's team sat in the grass. He watched Chelsie go up to kick. Green shirt billowing, she stood behind the white plastic plate, her legs bent, her body leaning slightly forward. Her eyes were fixed on the ball in the pitcher's hands.

Anders Kent, the school's best kickball player, rolled

the ball toward her. The game was a tie, 8–8, with only seconds left before the bell rang.

Bryan chewed on the white end of a blade of grass. He wanted to cheer on Chelsie, but he didn't want to be that conspicuous. Everyone would think he liked her.

The ball rolled closer and closer to the base. Chelsie swung her leg back, as if to smash it. Then, when the ball was over the white plate, she kicked it gently with the inside of her foot and raced toward first base.

"A bunt?" Anders yelled, charging at the dead ball. "A stupid bunt! I should have expected that from a rat!"

Rat. The word dug deep under Bryan's skin. Anders said the word with disgust, with hate—as though Chelsie were something slimy!

Anders stooped to pick up the ball.

Bryan's eyes burned. He didn't think. He jumped up, and before Anders could even straighten, Bryan was running full speed toward him. He skidded to a dead stop directly in front of Anders.

Anders's face went blank. "What?"

Bryan clenched his right fist, slammed it into Anders's nose, and kept walking.

"Hey!" Kyle called. "Bry! What's going on?"

He walked beyond the playing field, then stopped, head pounding, knuckles sore. His arms dropped limply to his sides. The school bell rang.

Bryan turned.

Anders was curled in a ball, moaning and holding his nose. Blood spurted between his fingers and onto his white shirt.

Bryan was stunned at what he'd done. Was he going crazy? His breathing came in shallow spurts.

Kids flocked around Anders. They helped him to his feet and walked him toward the school, glancing back over their shoulders.

A distant plane droned.

Kyle stood by his side. "What was that all about?"

Bryan cleared his throat. His mouth was dry as dust. Just outside the school doors, he saw Chelsie, standing alone. "Anders thinks he's such a hot shot."

"What's new?" Kyle studied him. "But why'd you smack him?"

"You heard him, didn't you?" Bryan looked past Kyle. Mr. Ottenstad, the principal, was striding toward them in his striped shirt and red tie. "Whoa . . ."

"You really like her, don't you?" Kyle said, shaking his head, his back to the principal.

"Turn around," Bryan said. "I'm dead now."

Kyle pivoted. "Oh, hi, Mr. Ottenstad."

"The bell rang, boys," Ottenstad said, planting himself three feet from Bryan. "Inside."

Bryan started with Kyle toward the school, a deep breath of relief forming in his lungs.

"Bryan," Ottenstad called. "Meet me in my office."

Bryan nodded. At the school doors, no one was waiting.

Inside the principal's office, Mr. Ottenstad paced, his voice high and wiry. "Bryan, just what happened out there?"

Bryan sat, looked at his brand-new Nikes, his new jeans. He shrugged.

"Bryan Grant," Mr. Ottenstad ordered. "Look at me, please."

Bryan made himself look up. Imagining music for this scene, he tapped his right toe in staccato. He'd call it "The Executioner's Song."

"First day of school, Bryan," said the principal.

The air was warm and heavy, probably stale from windows being closed all summer.

"I know," Bryan said, matter of factly. What was he suppose to say?

"First day of school," Mr. Ottenstad repeated, "and you start it with a fight. That's not what I've come to expect from you, Bryan. Did something change over the summer?"

Yeah, this whole town has changed, Bryan almost blurted, but he didn't.

"Well?" Mr. Ottenstad said, probing. He stopped pacing and tapped his red pen against the edge of his desk. "What do you have to say for yourself?"

Bryan's mind whirred. He knew he'd gotten angry because of what Anders had said to Chelsie, ridiculing her bunt kick just because her family worked for Badgett. But why did he have to flatten Anders? He didn't have a good answer. One moment, he was siding with his father, the next he was on the other side, defending Chelsie. He didn't know if he'd done the right thing or not.

Maybe he'd inherited his father's hot hockey temper. Maybe it was as simple as that.

CHAPTER ELEVEN

The rest of the afternoon, nobody called Bryan a hero. Kids murmured as he walked by.

On his way to the restroom, Bryan overheard one teacher scolding a fourth grader. "Her name is Isabelle, not 'rat.' Is that clear?"

"But everyone calls . . ."

"I don't care. In my classroom you will not call anyone names."

On his way back to his homeroom, Bryan saw Emily Carter, a fifth grader, get escorted to the office by a teacher's aide.

"But I didn't try to trip him," she pleaded, tears streaming. "I was just stretching my leg out when he passed."

"That's what you said, but Gimmel's ankle is sprained. That's serious, Emily."

Five minutes before the bell rang, Mr. Ottenstad's voice came over the intercom.

"Our town," he began, "is experiencing a great deal of tension due to labor disputes. In the midst of this tension, Blue Ash Elementary will be a place of peace and cooperation. All students, whether they are new to our community or not, are part of our school. Any name-calling or fighting will lead to strict disciplinary measures. We must all work together to make our school a safe and positive place."

When the bell rang, Bryan bolted from his desk. He was lucky to have escaped Ottenstad with only a warning. If anything ever happened again, Ottenstad had warned, then Bryan's parents would be called in. That would make an interesting meeting, Bryan thought. Dad would raise his eyebrows, then scowl, wondering if Bryan had gone soft for a Badgett girl. Mom would be glad he'd stood up against name-calling, until she found out he'd leveled someone.

Buses lined the school sidewalk, ready to transport kids like sardines in bright orange cans. Bryan kept his eyes down as he passed the lines of students. The principal's office. What a way to start the first day of school!

Someone lightly tapped his shoulder. He turned. Chelsie, her face pink, pressed a white note, folded to a one-inch square, quickly into his hand. "Here."

Bryan shoved it in his pocket. "Uh, thanks. I gotta go." He raced away, like a marathon walker, keenly aware of the note in his right jeans pocket. When he turned the corner to his neighborhood, he yanked the paper out, unfolded it, and read:

Dear Bryan,
Thanks for standing up for me today. I'm sorry Anders got hurt, and I'm sorry that you got in trouble. You're really sweet.
Chelsie

Grasshoppers were clacking and buzzing everywhere

as Bryan walked the five blocks to his house. A two-inch green one landed on his jeans leg. He waited to see if it would drop off on its own, but it didn't. Sweet? Chelsie thought he was sweet? When he got home, he gently picked the grasshopper off his leg and set it on a tall red zinnia.

A school bus pulled up to his house. Josh and Elissa hopped down its steps, racing up the driveway to meet Bryan. Life for seven-year-olds sure seemed easy. Bryan took the key from beneath the flowerpot, opened the door, and stepped inside.

The house was quiet. Too quiet. He didn't mind that Mom worked, but he still preferred her home when he got there. Anyway, in an hour she would be finished with her work at school. "Okay, you guys," he said. "What do you want for a snack?"

"Sugar Pops!" Josh answered.

Bryan shook his head. "We're supposed to save that for breakfast."

"Popsicles!" Elissa shouted, dropping her pink and green backpack in the middle of the kitchen floor.

"Elissa, you know what Mom would say," Bryan said. He put his hands on his hips, just like Mom would do. "Put that away."

Elissa, her hair in two tight braids with purple bows, gave him a pouty smile.

"That smile doesn't work on me," Bryan told her.

Elissa half closed her eyes and glared at Bryan. She picked up her backpack and danced it down the hallway.

Josh followed with his pack. When they returned they sat on the counter stools, waiting.

Bryan didn't feel like baby-sitting, even if it was only

for an hour. He'd rather go biking with Kyle and maybe see Chelsie somehow. "Hey," he said. "I know what we should do. . . ."

He went to his room, climbed up to his top bunk, and removed four dollars from the blue mason jar on his shelf. Reaching into his pocket, he pulled out Chelsie's note and read it once more. Then he carefully refolded it, dropped it into the jar, and screwed the lid on tight.

He returned and laid the bills on the kitchen counter in front of the twins.

Josh nearly touched his nose to the money. "Where'd you get so much money?"

"Here's the deal," Bryan said. "Since I have to baby-sit, bike with me wherever I want to go, and I'll treat you each to a cone at Dairy Queen."

"Are we biking to that *girl's* house?" Elissa asked. Her expression was sly.

"What girl?" Bryan asked, playing dumb.

"That girl that came by the other day. The one I saw diving on the video."

The video. He'd forgotten all about it. He'd have to watch it later.

"Do you like her, Bry?" Elissa continued.

"No way," he said, lying.

They biked to Kyle's house, then all four rode to Dairy Queen, where Bryan plunked down his money and bought cones. When they were finished, Bryan swung his leg over his bike seat. "Let's just bike down that way," he said, pointing to the southeast end of town.

"Why?" Kyle asked. "Does Anders live that way?"

"No." Bryan tapped his fingers on his handlebars. "Just follow."

Kyle raised his eyebrows. "Now I know. . . ."

"Ooooh," Elissa teased. "I bet *she* lives that way."

They rode single file along Highway 53, turned left, and wove through the neighborhood, Bryan leading.

A block away from the address Chelsie had given him, Bryan spotted two parked police cars. The street looked entirely different during the day.

"Hey!" Josh said, biking up next to Bryan. "Neat! Let's go find out what happened!"

"Think somebody died?" Elissa asked worriedly. Since last fall, when one of her classmates was killed in a car accident, Elissa always jumped to the worst conclusion.

"Course not," Bryan answered, but he suddenly felt sick. Why were police cars there?

Slowly, he followed behind Kyle, Elissa, and Josh toward the police cars. Outside the small cream-colored house, three policemen stood talking. One held a clipboard. A woman walked alongside the house with a notepad—it was Nancy Benton from the newspaper.

What had happened? Something bad, that was certain. Where was Chelsie?

Another police car pulled up next to the house and parked.

Bryan stopped pedaling. He glided slowly past, stopped, and looked over his shoulder. The inside of the house windows were painted with strange letters. The words were backwards. He deciphered the lettering in two windows: GO HOME! and NO MORE RATS!

He clamped his hands on the handlebars and spun the bike back toward the house.

"Hey," he called to the group of men. "Where's Chelsie Retting? What happened?"

"Are you a friend?" the police officer with a clipboard asked, his bald head reflecting the late afternoon sun.

Bryan nodded. "Yeah, I guess."

"She's all right. I can tell you that much," he said, his face somber.

"Where is she?"

The man turned away, then back again. Quietly, he answered, "Holiday Inn. Better run along."

Bryan pointed his front tire back toward Kyle and the twins, who waited at the corner. Just then, Sheriff Hunter stepped out of the house. Bryan pushed down hard on his pedal. He didn't want to talk to the sheriff.

Bryan persuaded Kyle and the twins to follow him to the hotel. The quickest route led Bryan past the housing camp. He biked ahead, fast, tires humming over pavement. He didn't look at the guardhouse, though he was positive that someone was watching him. He stopped at the corner and waited for the twins to catch up.

"Don't go so fast!" Josh whined.

At the Holiday Inn, where green neon lights trimmed the top of the two-story brick hotel, Bryan set his bike against the wall under the canopy roof. He pulled open the double doors to the lobby.

Kyle, Elissa, and Josh followed.

"Can we go swimming?" asked Josh. "Mom said this year we can have our birthday party here, and we can invite ten kids. I get to pick five friends. I'm going to pick Eric, Carsten, Daniel . . ."

"Josh and Elissa," Bryan said. "Just be quiet and sit down, okay?" He pointed to the black floral loveseats. Josh dove for the glass dish filled with white cellophane-wrapped mints.

"Just one," Bryan said. "Kyle, can you watch them, just for a minute?"

Kyle cocked his head at Bryan. "For two minutes. Bry, this feels really weird. What if we get kicked out?"

"Just say you're waiting for someone." Why did this have to be so difficult?

Bryan walked over to the front desk.

"Yes?" The woman wore a brass name tag engraved, Bitsy.

"I'm looking for Chelsie Retting. What room is she in?"

"I'm sorry," the woman said, pushing back the cuticles on her perfectly oval red fingernails. "I can't give you her room number, but I can call her."

Bryan nodded. This would be a good time to bolt out the door. He pushed his tongue against the roof of his mouth, then wet his dry lips.

"Your name?"

"Bryan Grant," he said.

The woman adjusted her glasses and lifted a phone to her ear. "There's a Bryan Grant in the lobby to see Chelsie. No," the woman said, eyeing Bryan. "He's just a boy."

The counter suddenly seemed to tower in front of Bryan. He felt small. All the courage he'd had suddenly dribbled away, just as if he were back in first grade. His cheeks burned and his vision blurred. He turned away from the desk and walked toward the lobby entrance doors.

CHAPTER TWELVE

"Bryan?"

Bryan heard Chelsie's voice, warmly familiar, but he didn't turn around. He could sense her moving toward him, coming from the hallway beyond the end of the counter. Her room must have been the first one down the hall.

Bryan stopped. He couldn't face her yet—he could barely think. Then he turned around.

Chelsie's face made him think of a bowl of perfectly ripe peaches. "So why are y'all here?" she asked, glancing toward Kyle and the twins on the couches. She stepped a few inches closer and whispered, "Did you hear what happened?"

Bryan nodded. But why had he come? Why, exactly? To see if she was okay? She was. To hear what happened? Maybe. To make himself feel less guilty? He didn't know.

"I was out biking and I saw police cars by your house. . . ."

She folded her arms over her chest and clasped her elbows.

"It looked like there was trouble," Bryan said.

She nodded, then spoke in a whisper. "Someone broke

into our house while we were at school. Mom came home from her shift and found the beds ripped to shreds and furniture smashed. They even cut up family pictures!" She glanced toward the ceiling. "They wrote swear words all over our walls. She picked me up from school so I wouldn't see it." She looked back at Bryan, with eyes that were completely trusting. "I'm so scared. Dad says it's enough that we have to put up with high rent . . . a thousand dollars a month . . . just to stay there. . . ."

A thousand dollars? Were locals charging that much to live in those tiny houses?

Chelsie continued, " . . . and then to have it destroyed."

Bryan wanted to reach over and touch her shoulder, the same as he would if one of the twins got hurt. But he didn't.

Her chin twitched. "Cam was doing so well," she continued, "and now he isn't talkin' again."

"What do you mean, isn't talking?"

"He's different," she explained. "Learning anything has always been hard for him. He didn't learn to tie his own shoes until he was eight. He makes progress; it's just a lot slower than normal—whatever that is. Anyway, movin' around every year hasn't helped. He makes a little progress, then slips again." She crossed her arms tighter. "This attack is really hard on him."

Tears shaped at the edges of her gold-flecked eyes, then her face crumpled. She pressed her hand to her mouth, turned quickly away, and ran toward the hall.

The woman with the wire glasses watched her, then glared at Bryan.

"Young man," she said, scowling, "I think it's time for you to leave."

• • •

72

Bryan chomped into a cob of yellow corn at the dinner table.

"Hey, Bry," Dad said, his deep voice filled with raw energy.

Bryan glanced at Dad and found he couldn't look him squarely in the eyes.

"I read your letter to the editor in tonight's paper. Nice job." He pushed his fist into the air and saluted Bryan with a thumbs-up. But the way he gave him the thumbs-up, without smiling, with such force, made Bryan want to shrink away. Sometimes Dad pushed too hard. Bryan was glad that corn kernels were wedged in his teeth so he didn't have to answer.

Bryan remembered the Hawks game when Dad, red-faced, had shouted into Bryan's helmet, "Get out there, Bry! Dominate the game!" Bryan had gone for the puck and forced his way into the middle of three Hawks—then had suddenly felt the slam of a hockey stick into his knee, felt himself going down under a dozen slashing blades. He'd ended up on the ice in the fetal position, crying, until Dad helped him off the ice. Bryan had hardly dominated the game that time.

Maybe writing the letter to the paper hadn't been such a good idea. Was Chelsie reading it right now? What would she think? He had thought he understood everything so clearly then, before he met her and Cam, before he understood that rats were just people, like him.

Mom passed the plate of ham steaks to Bryan.

"I love corn on the cob!" Elissa said. "Could we save a few kernels and plant them in the garden? Then we could grow our own corn next summer."

"Sure, Elissa," Mom replied. "We'll have to get some

dry seeds, but that's a terrific idea, honey."

"Dad," asked Josh, "are we really going to have our party at the Holiday Inn?"

Bryan kicked Josh under the table. If he mentioned anything about Chelsie, he'd be dead.

"Well," Mom answered for him, "it just depends. Maybe we should think about a party at home this year. You know, wait and see."

She looked at Dad.

"Stan," she said, "I heard at school today that Marsha Finney's husband got a new job. You know how long he's been looking?"

"No," Dad replied.

"Most of the year. He couldn't find anything. Going on Marsha's paychecks alone, and you know those teacher-aides don't earn enough to support a family." Mom looked at her plate. She paused.

"Stan, he got a job with Badgett." She spoke firmly.

Dad didn't look up.

Mom inhaled deeply and continued. "Seems there are quite a few people from town who are getting hired by them. The pay's not as good as with the union, of course, but it's not so bad."

Bryan looked at Mom, then Dad, to see if World War Three was about to start. He didn't say a word.

Dad's mouth was full. He chewed and chewed and chewed.

"Well, my point is," Mom said, setting her fork carefully on her plate, as if it might break. "It's not just out-of-town people now who are working for them. Things aren't quite so black and white anymore, you know what I mean?"

Dad finished his ham. He ate his corn. Through the rest

of dinner, he just stared at his plate. The silence was like steel, cold and impenetrable. When Dad's plate was empty, he pushed his chair back from the table, walked out the kitchen door to the garage, and started his truck. The engine's rumble filtered into the dining room.

Mom pressed her fingers to her temples. Her diamond ring caught light from the overhead brass chandelier. "I didn't want to make him upset," she said, looking at Bryan, "but he needs to see both sides."

Both sides. Bryan understood exactly what she meant. He knew what his dad felt. He knew what Chelsie felt. He just didn't know how *he* felt.

Numb. Maybe that was the word.

Suddenly, the door from the garage flew open. Dad stood there, wild-eyed. The truck grumbled behind him.

"I almost forgot. Tomorrow," he warned. "Don't go anywhere. Stay home."

Mom looked up. "Stan?" she said, rising from her chair. But he was already gone, the door slamming after him. Truck exhaust wafted into the dining room.

Mom grabbed the door handle. "Stan! You can't just tell us to stay home without any explanation. Stan—wait!"

Bryan looked through the white living-room sheers to the street. Dad's truck backed up onto the road, then raced toward town.

The truck's rumbling grew faint.

Mom stepped inside. She closed the door softly behind her and leaned against it.

"Mom, does that mean we can watch cartoons tomorrow?" Elissa asked. Her face was eager. "All day?"

"Yeah, can we?" Josh echoed.

"No," Mom said, her voice distant, as if it were

coming from faraway, "certainly not."

Bryan's chin twitched, his nose tingled. He looked away from Mom and stared out the window. Why would Dad come back inside to tell them to stay home tomorrow? A Saturday? It didn't make any sense. Wasn't Dad going to be around? And why *should* they stay home? On Saturdays, Mom always went grocery shopping, and when Dad couldn't fish, Bryan and Kyle always got together. Something made him think of Chelsie at the hotel, scared, afraid to go back to her rental house. Afraid for her brother. Maybe Bryan should warn her, but about what?

"Hi, this is Bryan Grant. My dad said to stay home tomorrow and I just thought, well, you should stay put, too."

Right. That would sound completely logical to Chelsie.

Still, though he couldn't put his finger on it, he knew it deep in his own gut. Fear. He almost considered calling the sheriff, but about what? To say he was afraid not only for Chelsie, but also for himself, for his dad—for the whole town?

Thinking of Chelsie, he went downstairs where the twins were plopped like wet noodles in their purple beanbag-chairs.

"Hey guys," Bryan said, taking a video down from the shelf. "Here's one terrific show." He inserted it into the video player.

"Bry!" cried Josh. "You can't. We were here first!"

Kyle's voice came over the speaker, ". . . executed with tremendous skill . . ."

Bryan watched himself on the television screen. At the edge of the diving board, arms out, glancing toward shore, he started teetering.

76

Josh and Elissa laughed. Elissa pointed. "You're gonna fall!"

That's okay if they laugh, Bryan thought. Chelsie came next, and he loved everything about her, especially her hair and her muscular calves and the way she entered the water with barely a splash. She was perfect, or at least pretty close.

Who knows what she thought of him.

CHAPTER THIRTEEN

Bryan woke to the sound of trucks rolling past his house. Dawn spilled a hazy light through his green bedroom blinds. He stretched, climbed down the bunk ladder, and threw on a T-shirt and jeans over his underwear. The air was chilly. He cranked his window shut.

The kitchen phone rang once.

As Josh breathed noisily on the lower bunk, Bryan slipped out.

From the kitchen, he heard his mother.

"I know," she said. "Something's up. No. He didn't come home either." There was a long pause. "Sure, Brenda, I'll call if I hear anything. Thanks."

As Bryan walked closer, Mom hung up the phone, unaware of him, and walked into the living room. She sat next to Gretsky on the sofa, looking over her shoulder through the sheers to the street.

"Mom?" Bryan asked. "What's going on?"

Without turning, she flagged Bryan closer with her right hand. He sat down next to her. Gretsky rolled onto his back, legs up. Bryan scratched him softly.

On the street, pickup after pickup loaded with men,

78

three to the front, several riding in back, rolled down the street. One truckload was singing, though Bryan didn't catch the words.

From a red truck, a beer can flipped from the passenger window. It rolled down the street, clunking to a stop at the gutter nearest Bryan's driveway.

"Where are they going?" Bryan asked. The trucks were heading south. He jumped off the couch and opened the front door.

"Bryan!" Mom called. Her voice was a shrill whisper. "Get back here!"

He stepped out, his bare feet absorbing the cold from the cement. The trucks were rolling right through the stop sign at the end of the street and turning right—toward the Badgett housing camp.

Bryan's teeth began to chatter. He stepped back inside, closed the door, and turned the brass dead bolt. He shook his head.

"It doesn't look good," he said. "Is Dad out there?"

"Let's hope not," Mom said, curling her feet underneath her robe like a young child. She wasn't very convincing.

Bryan thought of what Grandpa had said. The strike of 1934 was part of Teamster history. Maybe this was history in the making. Maybe things had to come to a full boil somehow and then the unions would regain their footing. Perhaps this was one of those times in history that others would look back on later as a good thing, something that had to happen, something inevitable. Bryan thought of the filming he'd done at the beach. "Mom?" he said.

"Mhhm . . ."

"Can I go to Kyle's?" he lied. He'd repent later. "We

were going to film each other, if that's okay . . . and I'll take care of the camera. Promise."

She looked at him. Beneath her eyes, circles had formed. Maybe she'd make him stay home, like Dad had warned. She smiled, but it didn't reach her eyes. She was more tired than Bryan had realized.

"Oh, okay," she agreed. "Cut across the backyards. I don't want you out there." She nodded toward the street. "Call me or come back soon, okay?"

"Right." He leaned over and hugged her, feeling the softness of her terrycloth robe against his cheek. "Everything will be fine, Mom. Don't worry."

"Thanks, Bry."

He hurried to his room, pulled on his hooded sweatshirt and sneakers, and hurried downstairs to the family room. He didn't really believe everything would be fine, but somehow it had slipped out, the way his mom used to say it when she kissed a bruised knee. He wasn't just his father's son—he was his mother's son, too.

From the VCR, he pulled the videotape of Chelsie and inserted it into the video camera, figuring he had enough film to shoot another hour or more of footage. Then he headed back upstairs with the case's strap across his shoulder.

Before Mom could change her mind, he opened the sliding glass door to the backyard and stepped out. Nonchalantly, he wove around the yard to the front edge of the garage and looked out toward the street. A rusty light-blue truck rolled past. Two men, one with a belly that didn't fit inside his black jacket, sat on the tailgate. Bryan didn't recognize them.

An inner alarm went off, blaring a message to his

brain. Hurry. Run. But he sauntered, taking slow, deliberate steps. He walked into the garage, got his bike, and pushed it over the dewy grass past Josh and Elissa's playset. If Mom glanced his way, he wanted to look as casual as he did every other Saturday morning. Only difference was it was 7 A.M., instead of 9 or 10. He pushed across his backyard, past the sprinkler at the Grinkos', the ripe tomatoes in the Sheenans' vegetable garden, and the neatly trimmed hedge of the Andersons' yard. Bryan looked straight ahead, hoping no one would stop him and say hello, and pushed his bike onto the small dirt path that wound through the aspen woods toward the field where he and Kyle played. He knew that that was where the truckloads of men were heading.

A canopy of aspen leaves, some turning golden, flicked in the soft breeze. Aspen, the lifeblood of the paper industry, had replaced nearly all the virgin pine forests. Bryan had seen old black-and-white photos at the historical museum that showed Rainy River clogged with logs during the nation's building boom. But that was in the past. Now Blue Ash was a paper town. More than once, Bryan had wondered what it would be like to step back to when voyageurs paddled the lake country between huge pine trees that made aspen look like toothpicks.

That's what money smells like.

He thought of the mill tour he'd taken in June. Giant mixing bowls stirred wood pulp into something like Cream of Wheat and, with massive rolling pins, reshaped it into endless sheets of paper. Trees became reams of paper, stacks and stacks ready for shipping. After the tour, Bryan received his own ream of paper. He'd picked canary yellow.

The woods smelled of late summer, sweet with tall patches of lavender asters and goldenrod. A fallen aspen

81

blocked his path. Bryan hopped off his bike, lifted it over the trunk, then hopped back on and sped down the trail.

He remembered the bald eagle. Fishing on Rainy Lake with Dad one day, a bald eagle had dropped from its perch in a huge pine and bulleted toward the water, only yards from the bow of their boat. It swooped so close, Bryan had seen its yellow eyes. In one smooth movement, with wings wide, it hit the water with its outstretched talons and soared up to the top of another pine with a good-size walleye. Perched over its prey, it tore at the fish with its hooked beak. Dad shook his head and laughed. "He's doing better than we are." Then, for a long time, they floated on the glittering water, watching the eagle. Dad whispered, "Isn't he a beauty?"

Heading down a slope, Bryan neared the ramp that he and Kyle had built. He flew over the wood sheeting, both tires off the ground for an instant, and landed beyond the wood block marking their furthest jump.

He glanced at the tree house, painted camouflage green and brown, its platform eight feet off the ground and supported by three aspen trees. Dad had helped Kyle and Bryan build it two years ago, when Dad had more time. Before everything had changed.

Bryan zipped past the tree house.

Why did everything have to mean choosing? Why did it have to be all one way or all another? Someone's loss, another's gain. Union or nonunion. Win or lose. Wasn't there a middle ground?

The sun was chasing away the night chill, scattering golden carpets on the forest floor.

Bryan hunched toward his handlebars. Ahead, beyond the edge of aspen, trucks lined the road next to the housing camp.

CHAPTER FOURTEEN

Over a hundred men were gathered on the street outside the housing camp. Bryan walked his bike off the path and into dewy goldenrod and grass, soaking his jeans. He tried to make his motions casual, natural. He didn't want anyone to notice him, especially his father.

Twenty, maybe thirty yards from the road, he put down his kickstand and squatted in the weeds, watching.

Some men sipped from white Styrofoam cups. Most looked edgy, glancing back and forth, milling about, as though they needed a leader.

Bryan took a breath. This wasn't frightening, not the way the passing trucks of men had made him feel. He'd overreacted. He took the video camera from its case, removed the lens cap, and lifted the camera to his shoulder like a news reporter.

A van with a camera on top and KBLH NEWS painted in rainbow colors across its side drove slowly from the west, from the direction of the Border Mall and Pizza Hut, toward the crowd. It wove around the men on the street. Bryan had the right idea. This was "history in the making." He pressed the "on" button. The camera buzzed next to his ear.

He spoke. "September ninth . . . history in the making . . ."

He stopped talking. He'd rather watch and film. Kyle could do it better, he'd find some way to make it all sound funny.

Inside the housing camp, two men stood by the guardhouse. Bryan recognized the wide-shouldered man—the hired bulldog—taking shelter behind the closed steel gate. Beyond him, two blue charter buses were parked. The housing camp looked strangely quiet. Saturday morning. Were all the Badgett workers still sleeping?

A dozen law enforcement officers paced back and forth inside, all wearing protective helmets. All, except one. Sheriff Hunter. The sheriff talked with the police officers on his side of the fence, then with the protesters on the other side. It was good to see the sheriff out there. He'd keep things under control. He hadn't needed Bryan's warning after all.

Minutes passed slowly. More pickup trucks pulled up alongside the curb. More men joined the growing crowd. Bryan shuddered. The sheriff's force looked smaller by the moment. If things got out of control, how could the sheriff and the small police force possibly hold back so many men?

The back of Bryan's throat burned.

The news truck edged down the street and stopped. A lean, long-legged man with wire glasses hopped out, springing ahead, his camera on his shoulder.

"Get that blasted camera out of here!" a man shouted.

Two burly men grabbed the newsman by either arm and dragged him back to his van. The camera crashed to the ground.

"Hey!" the newsman shouted as they shoved him toward the van. "You can't . . ."

Bryan's heart beat faster. He wiped his wet palms on his jeans, then tried to zoom closer to find the reporter's camera beneath the shuffling feet. It was gone. Why were they so uptight about cameras? Wasn't this a free country?

For a few more minutes, men milled about, as if at a friendly social. Then, as if responding to an unseen signal, they picked up gravel, just as Bryan had done, and pelted it over the fence at the mobile home windows.

Crack! Ka-ping! Crack!

Glass shattered. A mobile home window fell in shards to the ground.

"Stupid rats!" someone yelled.

Suddenly, a young mustached man from the group shouted, "Well, are we going to do it or are we just going to talk?"

He walked into the crowd, raising his arms into the air as if he were preaching a sermon. "Let's do what we came here to do!"

The crowd divided into two, one group pushing toward the fence, the other hanging back in the street.

"C'mon!" the man with the mustache yelled. "Let's get this job done once and for all! Are you a bunch of chickens?!"

Get what done? What were they going to do? Bryan bit down hard on his inner lip. He pressed the camera against his face.

One man, well over six feet tall, towered above the others. Bryan had seen him at the strike site once. He shouted in a deep voice, "It doesn't look like anybody's here, guys! We may as well go home."

"Hey, stupid! If you're not with us, then *you* go home! We don't need bystanders! Let's finish this job!"

Bryan bit too hard on his inner lip and tasted blood. His whole body tightened, as though it were a clam closing in on itself. He shrunk lower in the grass, dropping to his elbows and stomach. He crawled to a slope where he could look on, his zoom lens poking through the weeds.

One group of men stretched a line across a portion of the fence. "C'mon! Push!" The high metal fence bent slowly, as easily as an aluminum can. The men cheered, raising their fists high. "Rats go home! Rats go home!" The air was littered with four-letter words.

With war whoops, the men swarmed over the portion of downed fence that stretched twenty yards from the empty guardhouse.

On the edge of the street, yards away from the crowd, Nancy Benton, in a brown leather jacket and jeans, held a camera to her face. One of the strikers turned and pointed. Bryan wished he could warn her.

Three men strode toward her.

She lowered her camera and stepped backwards.

"No cameras!" one man yelled, tearing the camera from her neck and throwing it to the ground. He put his boot on it and glared at her. Nancy Benton spun away. She dashed to a silver car, scrambled in, and sped east, wheels squealing.

Trembling, Bryan reached over to his bike, yanked at the kickstand, and let it fall in the grass beside him. *Ka-thunk*. What would happen if someone found him filming? He eyed the woods. If he left now . . .

When he returned to his lens, the crowd looked like a giant amoeba—the kind he'd watched under a microscope in Mr. Crawford's science class last year—a single-cell organism that changed shape as it moved, flowing forward. Two men straggled behind and ran to catch up with the group. They looked over their shoulders nervously, as if someone might see them alone, knowing the group meant safety. In moments, the individuals blended in and disappeared.

Sheriff Hunter held a radio to his mouth as his handful of officers clustered together at the edge of the fence, like shy children on the edge of the schoolyard.

"Hey, Sheriff!" someone yelled. "Where's your National Guard, huh?"

National Guard? Were they supposed to help the sheriff?

Suddenly, the men swarmed around the mobile homes, wielding baseball bats that must have been hidden under their jackets. Bryan focused on the moving mass, a blur of legs and arms, relieved not to see his father among them.

For a few moments, the men moved out of sight, behind the first row of mobile homes. One yellow mobile home leaned slowly, rocking on its brick foundation, then crashed to its side. Dust and shouting filled the air. "We'll show those suckers!"

Bryan shook his head slowly, his mouth sour.

A group of men emerged from behind a mobile home and encircled a blue bus.

"Rock it!" From either side, they pushed, rocking the groaning bus back and forth. "There she goes!" On its side wheels, the bus hung for a moment, then creaked and fell to the ground with a slam. Men were laughing, slapping each other on the back and high-fiving.

Grass and weeds brushed against Bryan's camera lens as trucks rolled past, momentarily blocking his shot. A hornet hovered above his hand, buzzing, then flew on. How could grown men—fathers and grandfathers—do this?

Sitting up to a crouch, Bryan was determined to film as much as he could.

Men, increasingly jubilant, swarmed in and out of the mobile homes. One man, with a black cap and a red bandanna pulled over his face, swung a baseball bat at a glass window. It shattered to the ground, leaving a gaping hole. The man tugged at the rose curtains hanging there and pulled them outside. Then he reached down to the ground.

Bryan zoomed his focus closer. The man lifted a flaming rag to the curtains, lit them, and tossed the rag through the window. Within seconds, smoke seeped out the window. In less than a minute, smoke poured from the mobile home. As the man glanced toward the street, the bandanna fell from his face. Bryan focused right on the face.

It was Dad.

Bryan dropped the camera. He covered his open mouth with his hand and shut his eyes. His chest heaved with a silent cry. How could he? Was Dad crazy, too? He was the same as all the other men—hornets defending their hive, stinging their intruders, and killing themselves in the process. Bryan rose to his knees, grabbed a clump of weeds, and ripped it out by the roots. He flung it toward the street. So what if his father or anyone saw him! If his father could be part of this, then maybe nothing mattered anymore.

The camera buzzed in the ground, the lens in the dirt. Hands shaking, Bryan picked it up and brushed away dirt particles and bits of dried grass. He lifted it and refocused, but he couldn't find his father anywhere.

Flames burst skyward from the mobile home his father had torched, and from a dozen other homes in the camp. Smoke, gray and wispy, rose, slithering into the sky. It billowed into a dark pillar, fed by dozens of smaller fires, until it towered ominous and black above the whole town.

In the distance, sirens screamed, building to a deafening high pitch. Fire trucks sped around the corner from the west and zoomed toward the site. One fireman climbed out and stared. Then he raced with a hose toward the fire hydrant.

Within the camp, a dozen men approached an olive-green car. The car began moving. Men pelted the car with rocks as it increased speed and screeched through the open gate, its driver wide-eyed. In the passenger seat, the housing camp guard was slumped forward, hands pressed to his bloody forehead.

If they hadn't escaped, they would have been killed. Bryan knew it. If the Badgett workers had been there, many would have died. He shivered and flattened himself to the ground, the damp earth chilling his skin.

Small groups of men melded back into an amoeba again, into a mob, and flowed out of the camp through the downed fence. Bryan held his breath. He didn't move. If they decided to cross the field now, he'd be dead.

Finally, when voices and footsteps faded, Bryan lifted his head. He rose to cramped, stiff knees and unclenched his hands.

The amoeba moved away without anyone guiding it, moving slowly down the street to the west, then onto the highway. The mob grew smaller as it moved down the highway, between the community college and the Holiday Inn, with three police cars following slowly behind, as if they were at the tail of a parade.

Some parade.

When the mob continued on, not stopping at the Holiday Inn, but flowing toward the center of town, toward the mill, Bryan let out a shaky groan. All through his body and head, he felt badly bruised.

A fire engine roared from the east toward the camp, sirens shrieking. Beneath the black mushroom cloud, fire-fighters shot white arcs of water into smoke and flames.

On wobbly legs, Bryan stood up. His mouth hung open, dry and dusty, and the morning sun beat down on his head.

"Dad . . . ," he whispered.

CHAPTER FIFTEEN

Hand over hand, Bryan shimmied up the weathered rope to his old tree house. He couldn't go home yet. He needed time to be alone, time to think. Besides, how could he begin to talk, to act normal after what he'd seen?

He hoisted himself through the square opening and pulled himself up onto the wood floor. Crawling on his hands and knees toward the window, he took off his backpack and rolled onto his back.

An aspen branch sprouting yellow and green leaves poked through the crack in the corner, pushing apart the adjoining walls. The fort had taken two weekends to build with Dad's help. Now it was falling apart.

Flecks of gray rope fiber clung to Bryan's hands. He rubbed his palms lightly together over his chest, then stared at the flat ceiling.

A small black spider with a gray pouch crawled directly above him. Unflinching, Bryan watched it. Heck, what was a spider compared to a swarm of angry men? The spider flattened itself, motionless for a few seconds, then crawled slowly across the ceiling to a hairline crack and disappeared outside.

Through the window, morning light drew golden rectangles on the walls.

Bryan curled his legs up toward his belly, rolled onto his side, and tucked his head down. His eyes grew hot. He felt like a steam roller had crushed his ribs. From deep in his chest, a sob rose. He let it come, muffling his sounds with his knees.

Finally, when he felt like a wrung-out towel, he slept.

"Bryan?"

"Mmm . . ." Bryan opened his eyes and looked at the wood shelves he once hammered together, still holding some of his old paperbacks. Maybe the whole thing had been a bad dream.

"Bryan?" Kyle poked his bird's nest of blond hair through the opening. "Good, you're here. When your mom called to ask about you, I figured I better check here." He climbed up onto the floor. "She didn't sound too happy."

Bryan rubbed his eyes. If they were red, it didn't matter. "Did you hear what happened at the housing camp?"

Kyle nodded. "Who hasn't? The mayor was on the radio telling everyone to stay home. I saw smoke from my house! It was really incredible! I just biked by—what a mess! The place is destroyed."

"I watched the mob," Bryan said, his voice flat. "I saw everything."

"Yeah?" Kyle sat down, cross-legged, excitement in his voice. "And I heard those men went out to an apartment building where a family of a dozen nonunion workers lived. Somebody said a woman with a rifle kept them away, shouting at them in Spanish." Kyle shook his head. "Can you believe it? In our town?"

Bryan ran his hand over his backpack, feeling the edges of his video camera. If Kyle knew that Dad had been there, he probably wouldn't think much of his hockey coach anymore.

Kyle leaned forward. "My dad said the police escorted two busloads of men from town. Most of those guys were from out of state, so the town should be safe now."

"Yeah," Bryan said, not looking at him. It wasn't only men from out of town. He remembered Sheriff Hunter pacing behind the fence, trying to keep peace—and how he'd asked for Bryan's help earlier in his office. Bryan couldn't just let those men leave town without some sort of justice, not after what they'd done. He swallowed hard. "I got it all on videotape."

"You're kidding." Kyle's eyes grew wide. "Really? Let's go watch it."

Bryan crossed his arms over his chest and sighed shakily. "I'm in a mess."

"Why? What do you mean?"

"Kyle," Bryan said, "my dad . . . he was there."

Kyle winced and shook his head. "Boy . . . not good, huh?"

"I should turn the tape in to the sheriff, but if I do, I'll be turning my dad in at the same time." Bryan groaned.

"So . . . what are you gonna do?" Kyle asked.

Burrs covered Bryan's shoelaces and socks, brown puffs with a zillion feathery barbs. How could he turn in his own father? Dad was doing what he probably thought was right. But what if workers had been there, sleeping? Isn't that what the men had hoped? How far would Dad have gotten involved—to the point of blood? Standing up for the rights of the union workers was fine, but destroying

93

property, hurting others, didn't make any sense at all. Bryan picked off a burr and tossed it down the tree house hole.

Maybe he would toss the tape into the woods and pretend he'd never seen any of it. He remembered the shouts, "No cameras!" Of course they didn't want cameras! In large numbers, there was no way to identify them—except, perhaps, from the tape.

"Kyle," Bryan said. "Last year, when my parents went away for their anniversary, I watched a movie at my grandpa and grandma's. It was about Russia, following World War Two, when Stalin sent thousands of the Russian people to labor camps."

"Stalin? Who's he?"

"Like Hitler. Only in Russia. Anyway, children were encouraged to turn in their parents. Stalin didn't trust anybody—not even his own people. If children turned in their parents, the reds would . . . " He caught himself. " . . . the communists would praise the children."

"So?" Kyle screwed up his face. "I don't get your point. What's that got to do with anything?"

Bryan rubbed his forefinger above his lips, then clenched his hand into a fist. "Oh . . . don't you see? I can't turn in the tape. I'd be turning in my own dad!"

For another hour, they talked. When shadows filled the tree house, Bryan grabbed his backpack and pushed his arms through the straps. "Kyle," he said. "It's getting late. I better get going." He shimmied down the rope, Kyle following.

CHAPTER SIXTEEN

Bryan parked his bike in the garage next to his dad's truck and stepped over a small puddle of oil. What was he going to say to his father? How could he ever talk to him? He stopped by the door. Heart racing, he walked over the dirty welcome mat and stepped inside.

"Bryan?" Mom walked into the kitchen, a textbook in hand, her eyelids puffy. "Bryan . . . you didn't call. I've been worried sick."

Bryan kicked off his shoes and put them next to his father's boots. The television hummed downstairs.

"Where's Dad?" he whispered.

Mom's lips drew a pencil-straight line. Beneath her gray sweatshirt, her chest rose slowly and fell. "Well . . . he came home about an hour ago," she said, her voice wielding a steel edge. "He's sleeping now." She walked to the kitchen window. "Where's that stupid dog?! I let him out and now he's gone!"

It wasn't like Mom to call Gretsky stupid.

Bryan glanced at the clock on the stove. "Dad's sleeping? But it's only 5:30."

"He was exhausted," she said, not looking at Bryan. "I don't think he's slept in days."

"Where are the twins?" Bryan asked. His stomach grumbled as he reached for the blue-speckled cookie jar. He lifted the lid and looked inside. Empty.

"They're staying overnight at Grandpa and Grandma's. I just didn't know what to expect around here. I'm sure by now you've heard about the town and . . ."

A high-pitched yelp came from the backyard.

Bryan started, then sprang to the sliding doors just in time to see a black-and-white-striped creature, its fluffy tail flagged high, waddle slowly away from Gretsky and disappear into the aspen woods. Gretsky dropped to his forelegs. With his head to the ground, he batted at his snout, yelping.

"Gretsky got sprayed by a skunk!" Bryan shouted.

"Skunk? Oh great!" Mom said, looking out the window above the kitchen sink.

Bryan thrust open the sliding door. A pungent, putrid blast of air covered him like a sheet of heavy oil, filling his eyes, his nose, and his stomach. He wanted to throw up. Gretsky ran circles in the grass, stopping every few feet to paw his muzzle. Bryan wanted to help him, but what could he do? He stood there.

"Bryan! Close that door!" Mom yelled, her voice piercing. "Now the house reeks! If that *stupid* dog had listened, this wouldn't have happened!! A skunk! Terrific. That's just terrific!" Mom turned from the window. "He's out of this house for good! I've had it!"

"Mom, but it's not his fault!" Bryan shouted back, his eyes watering. "He didn't know better! He probably thought it was one of the twins' stuffed animals."

Gretsky scratched at the glass door. Bryan glanced

down at the dark, round, pleading eyes. "Look at him. He's miserable!"

He suddenly stopped yelling. His shoulders slumped. "Mom," he said quietly, facing her. His voice cracked. "Why are you being so mean?"

Mom scrunched her eyes shut and let out a shaky breath. "Ohhhhh. . . ." She shook her head slowly, stepped closer, and put her hands on Bryan's shoulders.

"I *hate* skunks, but it's not really about that. It's everything lately." She rubbed her forehead with her fist. "You see what just happened? I blew up at you and what good did it do? One person explodes, then the other explodes. All anger does is breed more anger."

Scenes of the riot, anger boiling over like a pot of scalding water, filled Bryan's mind. He looked at his mother's eyes, which had lost the craziness he'd seen just a second earlier.

"Anger is a choice," she stated, her palms up.

There was so much he didn't understand. Was anger really a choice? Or was it something that controlled a person, like instinct? From the other side of the glass, Gretsky whined. Bryan looked at him. Maybe Gretsky had acted out of instinct, going after the skunk, but if he had any brains in his head at all, he wouldn't go after another. Bryan swallowed, tasting the skunk's offensive odor.

Mom glanced at Gretsky and shook her head. "I don't know what we're going to do with him," she said, walking back toward the kitchen and grabbing her jacket from the peg by the door.

"Right now, I can't handle it. It's time for me to take a walk." Her voice wavered. "I need to burn off some of this stress."

97

"Mom?" Bryan asked.

She turned.

"Got any tomato juice? That's what the Sheenans used on their dog last fall."

"Downstairs," she said, "in the pantry. Flush his eyes with water, too. Thanks, Bry. I don't know what I'd do without you." For a second, the corners of her mouth lifted. Then she was gone.

Bryan put on the blue rainsuit he'd used only once for fishing and then went to rescue Gretsky, who now sat with his nose against the sliding glass door, whining. It was worse than the smell of the mill, worse than anything he could remember. "Here goes," he muttered.

Gretsky wagged his stub tail. *Aroo-woo-wooooo!* he moaned, as Bryan slid open the door.

"You really, really, really stink!" He held his breath and scooped Gretsky's sausage body under his arm. When his lungs started to burn, he let out his air in a blast, then inhaled deeply. "C'mon, brainless," he said. "Let's get you cleaned up."

Gagging and choking, Bryan carried Gretsky quickly, down to the basement and set him in the white laundry tub. He wet Gretsky down with warm water, lathered him in tomato sauce, and scrubbed him until he was completely red, except for his black button nose. Did Dad have a choice about anger? Could he have decided to stay home this morning?

As Gretsky licked the tomato juice, Bryan sank his fingers into the dog's coat, working the cool red liquid through the dense gray fur down to the dog's skin.

The picture of his father torching the curtain, the flames jumping out of control, haunted him. How could he?

How could his father actually destroy someone else's home? It went against everything he'd ever taught Bryan about good and bad, right and wrong. He'd also taught Bryan to stand up for himself, to make decisions, to be a leader. So now what was Bryan supposed to do? If he didn't turn in the videotape, there might not be any evidence against the other men. If he turned it in, he'd be going against his own father. His stomach twisted. It would never be the same between them again.

Gretsky suddenly shook his coat, splattering tomato juice all over Bryan's rainsuit.

"Thanks," Bryan rasped. "I doubt Chelsie would call you 'adorable' now."

Gretsky's swollen eyes streamed. He whined.

From above the sink, Bryan grabbed an orange plastic cup and filled it with cool water. He held the dog's muzzle firmly upward, then carefully poured a gentle trickle of water into Gretsky's eyes. The schnauzer blinked and struggled. "Hold still," Bryan said. "I'm only trying to help."

If Dad had a choice about anger, about getting involved, then he probably should have made it long before the riot ever started.

"I know one thing, Gretsky," Bryan said, his nostrils pinched painfully by the odor. "Going after that skunk was a real bad choice."

CHAPTER SEVENTEEN

After soaping, rinsing, and blow-drying Gretsky, Bryan blockaded him in the laundry room with the safety gate. The wooden frame and white plastic mesh of the gate made him remember when the twins were small and Mom penned them with her in the laundry room, the dryer whirring, the air warm and lemon-scented. He used to play peekaboo through the gate, making the twins giggle while Mom folded clothes. It seemed so long ago.

He scratched Gretsky between the ears, left him, and walked slowly up the stairs. He suddenly felt afraid. If Dad woke up and they started talking, maybe Dad would fly out of control. After today, after what Dad had done at the housing camp, how could Bryan ever trust him?

Tiptoeing quietly across the kitchen floor and down the hallway, Bryan passed his parents' bedroom. Through the shut door, he heard Dad's breathing. He was asleep.

Bryan went back to the kitchen, ladeled a bowl of stew from the stove, and ate. Though it was still early, he was exhausted.

He walked to his bedroom, set his backpack at the foot of the top bunk, and climbed up. With his clothes on, he crawled under the covers and closed his eyes, waiting for sleep to come and cover up his confusion. For nearly an hour, he tossed and turned, opening his eyes and glancing at his backpack, then shutting them again.

In his mind, the men's shouting and swearing filled the air. He pictured them with their bats stretched high—then their bats turned to stones. Crack! Ting! He remembered his own stones, flung with a solid aim at the guardhouse. Why did he think he was any better than the rest of them? His actions had been wrong, too.

Last Sunday, the scripture reading had been about the crowd that gathered in the dusty streets, shouting, "Stone her! Stone her!" at the weeping woman who lay crumpled on the ground. The shouts grew louder and louder. Suddenly, the crowd quieted. Nearby, drawing in the dust with a stick, was Jesus. The men held their stones high, waiting for him to speak. Finally, he rose to his feet and faced the angry crowd. "Whoever is without sin," he said, "throw the first stone." The men lowered their arms and dropped their stones. One by one, they slipped away.

Maybe some things weren't for kids *or* adults. Maybe this whole union battle wasn't about winning or losing, but about loving your neighbor, about simply dropping the stones.

Dad, if only you'd walked away. Things could have been different.

When the kitchen door opened and Mom's feet softly swept the hallway, Bryan closed his eyes again and tried to sleep.

When he climbed down his bunk ladder the next morning, Bryan's legs trembled and his stomach growled. What day was it? Sunday? It seemed impossible that only one day had passed since yesterday morning.

The sound of a spoon clinking against the side of a cereal bowl came from the kitchen. He pulled on jeans and a sweatshirt, and stood behind his closed door a moment, hesitating. How could he face his father? But sooner or later, he'd have to. He stepped out, used the bathroom, and walked down the hallway toward the kitchen. The house was filled with the fragrance of skunk.

In their terrycloth robes, Dad and Mom were at the dining-room table with their cups of steaming coffee.

Dad was slouched forward, holding his white cup in both hands, as though warming himself on a cold winter morning. His skin was gray, hair rumpled, and face unshaven.

Bryan cleared his throat. His parents had never looked so tired. "Hi."

Dad glanced up, not lifting his head. He didn't say a word.

"Good morning, Bry," Mom said. "Want some cereal?"

"Sure." He sat down, poured himself a bowl of Life cereal, and set the box in front of him, pretending to study the maze on the back. He wished he could find a simple way out of the mess he was in. Could he forget all about what he'd recorded on the tape? Could he just do nothing? The videotape was a powder keg waiting to be ignited.

A car pulled into their driveway. The engine quieted and one car door, then another, opened and slammed shut. The doorbell rang. Gretsky jumped off the couch and started barking.

Bryan looked around the corner of his cereal box at Dad. He didn't move; he just stared into his cup of black coffee.

Mom pushed back her chair, then brushed her hair with her fingers. She glanced at Dad, sighed, and went to the door.

"Good morning, Mrs. Grant." It was Sheriff Hunter. Standing behind him was another officer. "Is your husband here?"

Gretsky stood next to Mom, barking.

"Stan?" Mom whispered, turning around.

Bryan ducked behind his cereal box. He didn't want Sheriff Hunter to see him.

Dad rose from his chair and stood tall. He crossed his arms over his chest. "Hi, Carl," he said. His voice was low, without a trace of warmth. "What's up?"

"Stan," the sheriff said, "you are under arrest for arson, criminal damage, and rioting. You have the right to remain silent. . . ."

Dad's forehead furrowed into a mass of lines. "What?"

Sheriff Hunter continued reading from a slip of paper. "Anything you say can and will be held against you in a court of law. You have the right to have an attorney with you when you're interviewed. If you cannot afford an attorney, one will be appointed for you. Having these rights in mind, would you be willing to talk to us?"

"Hey, now you listen!" Dad said, punching the air with his right fist. "You can't come into my home and arrest me!" His chest heaved and his voice grew louder. "You're arresting the wrong man. I was born and raised here! You know that. It's those other guys, the rats, you should be going after!" He paused, his arms dropping to his sides, and spoke more softly. "Besides, what evidence do you have?"

"Eyewitness, Stan," the sheriff told him. "I wish I could say the same for the others. Most came from out of town."

Bryan hung his head, and chewed on his thumb knuckle. He felt like he was shrinking, growing smaller and smaller in his chair. He couldn't believe this was happening. And how could his father think he was innocent? How could he defend himself? When Mom stepped to Bryan's side and placed her hand on his shoulder, something broke within him. He couldn't be strong for her, too. He slipped from the table and ran to his bedroom.

"Can I get dressed?" he heard his father ask, almost in a whisper.

CHAPTER EIGHTEEN

After the footsteps were gone and the sheriff's car pulled away, Bryan heard his mother crying. Eventually, he'd talk to her and tell her what he had seen, but he needed time. He stood in front of his bedroom mirror and saw a frightened boy staring back.

No matter how much he loved his father, he still hated what he'd done. And he resented that his father had put him in this position. He remembered a game when he was stranded by the home net, left alone against the opponents with sticks and blades and ice shavings flying. His father had shouted from behind the boards to the rest of the team. "Help him outta there!"

Bryan felt stranded now.

Help me outta here! Dad, help me out.

For much of the day, Bryan's mom was on the phone, arranging a community church service. In mid-afternoon Bryan spotted her resting on the hammock.

Easing open the sliding door, he inhaled the spicy scent of marigolds and walked past Gretsky, who was staked out on his chain, whining.

Bryan swallowed hard and touched the edge of the hammock. "Can we talk?"

Mom glanced up and nodded, her eyebrows raised questioningly. A breeze rushed through the arching willow branches.

"When will Dad come home?" he asked.

"I don't know." Her voice was flat. "As soon as I post bail," she said. She closed her eyes and pressed her middle finger and thumb against the bridge of her nose. "Right now," she continued, her voice rising, "I'm so angry—and hurt—I just want to let him sit there and stew!"

She turned to Bryan. "Why am I the one who's supposed to pick up the pieces after him? Why should I scramble to find bail money?"

Bryan opened his mouth to respond—though he didn't know what he'd say—then closed it. She wasn't looking for an answer.

"I mean . . ." She laughed halfheartedly. "We certainly don't have a few thousand dollars just floating around."

She took a deep breath, then sighed in jagged descending steps. "How could he do this to us?!" she cried. "I just don't understand it!"

Brian was quiet.

Willow leaves cast flickering gray shadows on her face.

"Mom," Bryan said finally. "I have a few things to tell you." He told her about the stones and following Dad on his bike the night of the tacks episode. And then he told her about the videotape and seeing Dad at the riot.

Tears pooled in her eyes. "You'll have to talk to him," she said quietly. "He needs to know."

• • •

That evening, the church was packed. Bryan looked around. The sanctuary was lit with candles, casting a golden glow toward the dome ceiling. The church was packed.

"We need to take a hard look at our community, at its wounds, and to find ways to bring healing. . . ." The words flowed from the pulpit.

On either side of Bryan, the twins squirmed. Bryan glanced at Mom, who looked straight ahead, slowly spinning her wedding ring around her finger.

" . . . this is about the Retting family—and others— who have lost their homes. We need to ask ourselves, each one of us: How can I help? Some of us have extra sleeping space in our homes. Others can provide a donation to help with replacing basic personal items. . . ."

Chelsie's apricot hair hung over the backseat of the first pew. Bryan sat behind her. Just looking at her hair made him feel a little better. On either side of Chelsie and Cam, who swayed his head slowly back and forth, even though there was no music, sat a woman whose long dark ponytail was tied back with a white bow and a man with a quarter-size bald spot. Most likely, their parents.

"Are you willing to help? Are you willing to be part of the healing this town needs? If so, raise your hand. . . ."

Bryan thought about his own part in the violence— throwing rocks and later tackling Anders. He couldn't change what he'd done, but he could learn from it. He could at least start trying to be part of the solution.

Along with other hands going up all across the church, Bryan lifted his toward the ceiling. He'd help Chelsie and Cam in any way he could. But could he help Dad, too?

After the service, when others shuffled to the church basement for coffee, punch, and cookies, Bryan slipped outside and sat on the cement steps. The evening air was cool, scented with the marigolds that lined the church sidewalk, marigolds Dad had planted in the spring.

Bryan leaned forward and pressed his hands between his knees.

The sky was growing dark. From where Bryan sat, he could see the law enforcement building half a block away, illuminated by bright lights. Tomorrow, after school, he'd visit. Mom had agreed that he needed to visit alone, so after school, Bryan was to drop the twins at Grandpa and Grandma's. Maybe he'd stop by the library and pick up a book or two . . . or three . . . to help Dad pass the time. The trial, Mom said, could be weeks away.

Footsteps pattered behind him. Bryan looked over his shoulder.

"Hi," Chelsie said. "Mind if I join you?"

A few days ago, he would have fallen down the steps, tripping over his own tongue, but so much had happened. He shrugged.

"It was pretty boring downstairs," she commented.

Bryan inhaled hard and let out his breath again. He rubbed his finger above his upper lip. "It's better out here."

"Your dad's over there tonight?" Chelsie asked with a nod of her head.

Bryan didn't answer. How could she know so soon? "It's none of your . . ." He stopped himself.

"I'm sorry, but your mom just told me. She said it might be better if she told me than . . ." Chelsie brushed her hair back over one shoulder and sat down next to Bryan, close. She smelled—soft. "Your mom's nice."

He stared at his sneakers.

"How are you doin'?" she asked quietly.

He didn't really feel like talking, not now, but he turned his head and met her eyes. "It's been pretty tough."

"Yeah." She twisted her hair, working long strands between her thumb and forefinger into a tight, thin rope.

"Were you scared yesterday?" he asked.

She nodded. "My dad wished he'd gone out of town like the others. He said lots of them were going to stay and fight, but the sheriff ordered them out of town for the weekend. Everyone had to go."

"Except the guards," Bryan added.

"They were s'posed to leave, too, but they wouldn't. Just like the others, they wanted to stay and fight . . . that's what my dad said."

Behind them, the church doors opened. It was Cam and Chelsie's parents. "Time to go, honey," her mom said.

Chelsie stood up slowly. "See ya."

Bryan didn't move. "Chelsie?"

"Yeah?" She turned to face him as her family walked into the dark parking lot.

He cleared his throat. "There's open swimming at the high-school pool Tuesdays. Want to practice dives sometime?"

She glanced over her shoulder. "I've gotta go, but . . . I'll have to ask but . . . sure." Her face lit up like a candle and then she was gone.

"Good," Bryan called. "See you at school."

CHAPTER NINETEEN

The next day, a ragged curtain of gray hung above the southwest edge of town. After school Bryan biked with the twins to the senior citizen apartments, dropped them off, and stopped at the library. Then he biked around town, weaving up and down streets, pumping his pedals so fast that his thighs burned. How could he face Dad? A late afternoon wind whipped against his face, carrying the smell of a smoldering giant bonfire.

Finally, Bryan forced himself to bike toward the courthouse and jail. In front of the redbrick building, he hopped off his bike, pushed down his kickstand, and shoved his hands in his pockets.

All day at school, kids had talked about the riot, but Bryan had kept his mouth shut. And when he sat with Kyle and Chelsie at lunch, he was grateful that no one mentioned his father.

He kicked a stone off the sidewalk and sent it skittering beneath the sumac bushes. Next to a RESERVED sign, a dark car with the words FEDERAL BUREAU OF INVESTIGATION was parked. The FBI? Was the riot something they were getting involved in?

Bryan inhaled deeply. He pushed his shoulders back and opened the glass door to Koochiching County Law Enforcement, wondering how many men besides his father were behind bars.

He walked slowly up to the empty counter.

"We could have gotten killed out there!" someone shouted from a backroom. "The governor said he'd send the National Guard! So where were they?"

"Good question," someone else replied.

"One thing's certain. Crossing state lines means FBI involvement now. We'll need their help making arrests."

Bryan pressed the top of a silver bell. Ting!

A uniformed man with a sucker in his mouth came from the hallway. Noticing Bryan, he removed the red sucker and frowned. Shadows circled his eyes. "Hope it's important."

"I came to see my dad," Bryan said, his voice a shade above a whisper. His mouth was dry, his stomach hollow.

"Name?" The sucker went back in the man's mouth.

Bryan swallowed. He didn't want to have to say it. Saying it made it too real. He cleared his throat. "Uh . . . Stan Grant."

"This way."

Bryan followed, climbing a flight of stairs and running his hand along the steel railing. In the waiting room, the officer lifted a tan phone from the wall. "Family visitor to see Stan Grant," he said.

Behind a wall of glass, a woman with brown curls sat in a room filled with control panels and monitors. The woman studied Bryan. Lights flickered behind her. "You'll have to leave your backpack here," she said through a speaker. A metal drawer clunked open, almost into Bryan's knees.

"But . . . I have some books for my dad."

She nodded. "That's fine. We'll get them to him when you're done visiting." The drawer shut, swallowing Bryan's backpack. The woman pushed a button and the officer opened a nearby door marked JAIL.

First, the officer quickly frisked Bryan's sides, then he led him toward a well-lit booth with mesh-wire, bullet-proof glass. Three metal stools and three phones faced another room with stools and phones. Another glass wall divided the booths. It was just like in the movies, only this was real. He recoiled at the idea of talking with his dad through glass. With a sweaty palm, he touched the window and sat down. He wanted to hide.

"Ted," came a familiar voice from the hallway. Bryan looked out. It was Sheriff Hunter. "This once," the sheriff told the officer, motioning toward the booth, "let's make an exception."

The officer returned. "C'mon," he said and led Bryan to another room marked ATTORNEYS AND CLERGY. "Guess the sheriff trusts you."

The room with filled green vinyl lounge chairs, a table, pop and candy machines, and a dusty, plastic hanging plant. "He'll be here soon."

Bryan stood in the middle of the room.

The tournament game flashed in his mind. Start of the third period, they were ahead, 5–4. Bryan raced out on the ice, stick ready, fired up. He held his stick down, facing off at center. The referee dropped the puck between Bryan and the opposing player. Bryan rammed his stick at the puck, missing it. Someone clipped him from behind, spinning him in a circle. He took off again, all his energy focused on the puck as it skidded between skate blades. He darted after the

112

puck with his stick, stole it, and slammed it across the white ice, straight toward the net's right corner and under the goalie's nose. The moment the crowd went crazy, Bryan noticed the goalie's familiar red and white uniform. Chip, the goalie, raised his mask and stared at Bryan. Oh no! By mistake, he'd scored on his own team!

Eyes burning, head down, Bryan skated slowly off the ice. How could he have been so stupid?! He pushed through the swinging half-door into the player's box.

"Good one," said Kyle. "Bet they appreciated that."

"We *were* ahead," Tyler added with a low groan.

Dad rested his hand on Bryan's padded shoulder, stopping him from sitting down on the bench.

"Listen up!" he said, looking Bryan straight in the eyes. "We all make mistakes sometime!"

"Not like that!" Bryan shouted back.

"Get back out there! Skate hard! Do your best!" he shouted above the din in the arena. Firmly he turned Bryan by his shoulders back to face the ice. "We need you!"

In the last four minutes of the game, Bryan fired the two winning shots. The crowd cheered. Mom and the twins waved red flags from the front row. They'd won, 7–5.

Footsteps filled the hallway.

Bryan turned. Dad stood in the doorway. His face was shaved, his dark hair combed. "Hi, Bry," he said, his voice warm but uncertain.

"You go ahead and visit," the officer said. "I'll let you know when your time's up."

Bryan glanced at his father, who framed the doorway, looking at him. "May I come in?" his father asked, adding a chuckle that fell flat.

Bryan looked away. He wanted to look his father in the

eyes, but he couldn't. He walked over to the barred window and stared at his freckles in the glass.

Chewing the inside of his lip, Bryan kept his hands in his pockets. "I brought a few books," he said, "two Sherlock Holmes mysteries, a *Star Trek* book, and another called *Coaching Hockey*. I thought you might want something to read."

Vinyl squeaked as his dad sat down. "Thanks."

Bryan didn't move.

"Putting the wrong people behind bars," Dad said. "It's not justice at all. Arresting the wrong people in this one, that's what I say."

Bryan's neck and face burned hot. He couldn't take his father's blustering. He looked at his own eyes in the tinted glass, glass that you could see out through, but others couldn't see in. He had to tell his father the truth. He had to be honest. Bryan couldn't stand it anymore. "Dad," he said, "I was there. I saw it all."

The room was quiet, except for muffled voices from somewhere else in the building. Bryan waited for an explosion.

"You were there?" Dad's voice came quietly.

Bryan nodded, gazing out the window.

"Well . . ." Dad seemed to force cheeriness into his voice. "What did you see?"

"Everything," Bryan whispered, his neck and shoulders tightening. "You."

A heavy silence filled the room.

Turning slowly, Bryan looked first at the tiled floor, then back at his father. Dad shifted in the chair. He held his head in his hands. Now that Bryan had started, there was no turning back. He spoke in a rush. "I was in the field across the street. And now I have this problem, because I had the video camera, and I got it all." His voice rattled. "I got everything on tape."

Dad groaned. "You were there. . . ."

"Tell me what to do, Dad." Bryan's voice grew louder. "You've always told me to stand up for what's right and I know I should turn this in . . . but you're on the stupid tape with all the others!" His hand trembled against his jeans.

His father sighed and rose heavily from the chair. "I never thought . . ." He rested his warm hands on Bryan's shoulders.

Bryan's pain curled into fists. He flung his father's arms aside. Head down, he threw himself forward and drummed his father's chest. "You shouldn't have been there! You shouldn't have . . ." His voice faded.

He felt his dad close his hands around his own, holding them still. He let his father draw him into the familiar smell of his flannel shirt, his skin. "I never thought," Dad said, his voice muffled in Bryan's hair, "I was capable of going so far."

Bryan's head pounded, and he closed his burning eyes tight. The smell of skunk still clung to his skin.

"I've really tried," Dad said, "but look where I am. I couldn't sleep last night, just thinking about what could have happened. What did happen."

Voices floated through the hallway. A fly buzzed against the window.

Dad cleared his throat. "Listen," he said quietly. He stepped back, shrugging his wide shoulders. "If that tape's evidence, then it's against the law to withhold it. You know what you have to do."

He let out his breath, long and slow. His square chin

quivered. "More important, Bry . . . is what I've done to you. You stood by me—even wrote that letter to the paper—and I let you down. Big time."

"It's not just you, Dad," Bryan said. "I threw stones at the guardhouse, too . . . all on my own."

Bryan hugged his father fiercely, forcing down the hot ball rising in his throat. He knew he'd changed, grown, in ways he couldn't fully understand, in ways he couldn't explain to his father. Someday he'd figure it all out. And someday he'd tell his dad to get back out there and try again. But not right now. Not yet.

Some things would take time.

AUTHOR'S NOTE

Though a work of fiction, this story is based on events that the author lived through in International Falls, Minnesota, on September 9, 1989, when a labor dispute erupted in a riot, gaining national media attention. Fifty-eight arrests were made following the riot, resulting in misdemeanor and felony charges.